D0963243

THE SEX OFFENDER

ALSO BY MATTHEW STADLER

Landscape: Memory
The Dissolution of Nicholas Dee
Allan Stein

THE SEX OFFENDER

a novel

Matthew Stadler

GROVE PRESS
New York

Copyright © 1994 by Matthew Stadler

All rights reserved. No part of this book may be reproduced in any form or by
any electronic or mechanical means, including information storage and retrieval
systems, without permission in writing from the publisher, except by a reviewer,
who may quote brief passages in a review. Any members of educational
institutions wishing to photocopy part or all of the work for classroom use, or
publishers who would like to obtain permission to include the work in an
anthology, should send their inquiries to Grove/Atlantic, Inc., 841 Broadway,
New York, NY 10003.

Originally published in 1994 by HarperCollins Publishers, Inc., New York

Published simultaneously in Canada
Printed in the United States of America

FIRST GROVE PRESS EDITION

Library of Congress Cataloging-in-Publication Data

Stadler, Matthew.
    The sex offender : a novel / Matthew Stadler.
        p.   cm.
    ISBN 0-8021-3695-8
    1. Child molesters—Fiction. 2. Sex offenders—Fiction. I. Title.

    PS3569.T149 S48 2000
    813'.54—dc21
                                                    99-055843

Grove Press
841 Broadway
New York, NY 10003

00 01 02 03   10 9 8 7 6 5 4 3 2 1

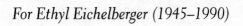

For Ethyl Eichelberger (1945–1990)

Without the generosity and intelligence of my editor Robert Jones this book would not be what it is. Thank you to Gloria Loomis and Nicole Araji for getting the book to Robert, and for doing practically everything else. The late George Stambolian gave important support when the text was still a mess. A Guggenheim Fellowship allowed me to finish the book. Thank you all.

THE SEX OFFENDER

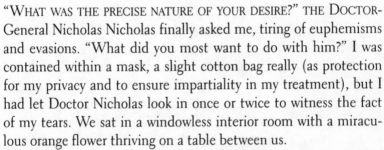

"WHAT WAS THE PRECISE NATURE OF YOUR DESIRE?" THE DOCTOR-General Nicholas Nicholas finally asked me, tiring of euphemisms and evasions. "What did you most want to do with him?" I was contained within a mask, a slight cotton bag really (as protection for my privacy and to ensure impartiality in my treatment), but I had let Doctor Nicholas look in once or twice to witness the fact of my tears. We sat in a windowless interior room with a miraculous orange flower thriving on a table between us.

"I wanted to open my mouth and swallow him. I wanted to swallow us both." The doctor jotted notes on a yellow pad and pushed at his glasses with the tip of a wooden pencil. He was smooth and dry, like a little seed or a dull white pill.

"Literally, swallow?"

"Yes, literally swallow."

He looked for a while, I'm sure, at my cotton bag. "Is it something you actually tried to do?"

"I would put whatever part of him that would fit into my mouth."

"And would you, then, bite?"

"I would use my teeth, on occasion, to create a, a . . . "

"A wound?"

"An excitement, a sensation. Like you might do with your wife."

He let his pencil rest and looked at me quizzically. "I don't understand, exactly." I took his hand in mine and put his finger in my mouth, lifting the bag, and sucked on it, softly, as I did with Dexter, and then I let my teeth tickle across its underside.

"Like that. Only sometimes harder and with his prick mostly."

"With his genitals?"

"Yes."

"Were you aware of the laws then?"

"What laws?"

My doctor is a four-star general. I made love with a twelve-year-old boy so I can't be a teacher anymore, but the general was so impressed by my unrepentant essays that he decided I should become a writer. I wrote about the sweetness of Dexter's skin when I licked it, the mingling of our tears when he fucked me, and my religious desire to love him more. The wise Doctor-General took me under his wing, orchestrating a baffling panoply of therapeutic practices, and granted me a new life, an opportunity to find my proper place in the greater social scheme, a chance to discover the right relation of love and, I guess, politics. I would be removed, taken away from the hazy relentless warmth of that southern metropolis (where my boyish love, Dexter, would remain) and sent back to the city of my youth, the capital of our northernmost province, cradled in the ancient mountains by the sea.

The train made the long journey without incident, shackled to its metal rails, the view out softened by rain. After the tea service I dozed off, subdued by the gentle rocking and my melancholy (an inevitable feature, for me, of train travel). I only awoke when we arrived and our forward motion ceased. It was dusk now, and clouds of steam billowed from the engine's belly into the cold air.

I gathered my few parcels and stepped out onto the platform. There were porters tacking briskly through the crowds, wheeling trunks and luggage on their clattering handcarts. I rubbed my eyes and looked up to see the day's last light draining through the dirty glass high above me. Rain beat upon the iron lattice. I took a few deep breaths of the wet air, with its familiar iron and salt smell. I was exhausted. Where were my trunks? The porter nearest me refused my tags, evidently put off by the red ministerial seal. His forearm rippled with a river of tiny muscles as he pushed the heavy cart past me. I slumped against the train, burdened by my one small overnight pack, and waited for my salvation.

And there he stood, dripping in a fashionably cut trench coat, just in from the rain. My Doctor-General Nicholas Nicholas, gazing at me in his silence. He'd come before me, on the previous day's train, to make all the arrangements and settle in—for the duration.

"We have your trunks," he began. "You needn't bother yourself about them." I fidgeted nervously, a little cowed by his well-creased trousers. He pointed toward the one trunk, indicating that it was mine, and took my hand to lead me out into the dusk.

If you were to fly by overhead, say in a balloon, I think you would find the city is shaped as an hourglass. Dipping down out of the clouds you'd see the deep harbor carving out the western hollow, the dark green hills cutting in from the east. The noise and filth of industry might reach you depending on the wind and your nearness to the valley of the gray factories (there above the capital's thin waist, running north like a waxy scar along the broken tracks of the railway). The sulfurous smoke of the foundries is a permanent condition of life here, mixing obscurely with the salty sea breeze and the rich, woodsy air. The wind coming through the valley carries it down among the houses, dusting the trees and children with a soft, silky ash. Tall mountains block our exit east.

The old center of the city lies like a patchwork cozy, lumped up on steep hills, crazy and cramped, with the central station pointing out from it into the valley of the gray factories. Even on bright days it can be enveloped in mist, and on the day of my return it was doubly so. The air touched me, soft and damp as a boy's hands, and I stared out into it, into the city. Everything was familiar to me: the old district, its opera house rising above the ramshackle lanes, the harbor busy with the noise and flurry of commerce. Newspaper vendors sitting in cramped kiosks rolled cigarettes and stared into the evening. The Doctor-General had two tram passes (one sporting my photo from the evening of my arrest) and an umbrella. Holding my hand, he led me across the empty plaza toward the "number five."

Mr. Nicholas, as he asked me to call him (for the sake of formality, I presumed), offered me the pass and a small package of related papers—maps, guidebooks, leases, etc. The key to my new apartment was included, with its address indicated on a small cardboard tag.

"Will I be living alone?" I asked. The tram had not yet come and we sat by ourselves on a wooden bench by the sign saying "5." My doctor did not answer. The bench was slatted, and damp from the mist, and I felt it press against me. We were silent together, wrapped in the evening. I stared at my dumb, unyielding face in the photo, remembering the grave instruction of the clerk by whom it was taken. "Act natural," he said. I had kept still, exhausted and a little puzzled as the flash burst open and blinded me.

A rumbling drew me away from this memory, and I looked up to see the big number five rattling out of the mist. My doctor was busy scribbling notes. He passed one to me (a prescription, by all appearances) and pressed it into my palm. "Reflect on your crime," he said, "and the events that have led you here.

"We'll meet tomorrow morning to talk." Then he ushered me onto the tram. I watched his small form disappear into the gloom and distance, and did as he had asked me . . .

It was the evening of my last offense. The arresting nurse lavished ink upon my fingers, taking prints, and handed me a lengthy form. I looked at the matronly officer, her sweet face enclosed in its cap, the evidence of my sexual mingling with Dexter clutched to her breast in a little bag, and I wondered just what sort of answers she wanted. "Corporal Johnson," I asked, noticing on her small metal badge this rank and surname, "would the Ministry prefer I go into some detail, or will a simple 'yes/no' suffice?" She sat stiffly on the bed's edge and surveyed the floor for more signs of my interrupted passions. I heard Dexter crying in the other room, and then the door closing as they took him from me.

"Detail, please," she said.

Fairness procedures were followed and I was given a number and a mask (as I've said before). There were other cases like mine and we were made to wait together before seeing the doctors for our first interviews. We wore green pajamas and the doctors wore white. The details of my life outside the actual activity of child molestation (as my love affair came to be called) were supposed to be kept out of court. I sat at a gray metal table and took pills and a glass of orange juice.

"Your essays intrigue me," Doctor-General Nicholas said as an icebreaker. Seven doctors sat at the raised wooden dais attended by nurses bearing water. Their shiny black shoes poked out below the clean frock of the wide, arcing desk. The humming of the fans was punctuated by their nervous drumming of pencils on the tabletops. Doctor-General Nicholas was in the very middle, slightly higher and more luminescent, I thought, than the others. "You seem to have thought a great deal about politics."

"Oh that," I gave back, disappointed that he'd chosen that from among the many essays. It wasn't my favorite. "I copied that, paraphrased it from a book I read."

"Do you read a lot?"

"I do. I read books for school."

"You're a student?"

"A teacher."

"You seem quite young to be teaching."

"I'm thirty years old. I've taught for five years now."

"Yes, I see that now, on the forms. Was the boy a student of yours?"

I hesitated, uncertain who "the boy" was. Silly, it was Dexter of course, and he *had* been a student of mine. "Yes. I taught Dexter history."

"Was he aware of your political positions?"

"No, I, I don't really have 'political positions.'"

"But your essay."

"That was simply an answer to the question, the question on the form. It's not really something I think about."

"What *are* your thoughts about politics?"

"I, as I said, I don't have any. It doesn't occur to me to think about it."

"And your crime, have you thought much about that?"

"My love of Dexter?"

"Your molestation of him."

"Our making love?" Their silence said go on. "Well, yes. I'm almost always thinking about sex with him. I was thinking of it just now, as you asked me about politics."

The line of white faces moved forward, as a wave lapping a little shore. The black shoes tucked neatly back, out of sight.

"You're imagining sex during the hearing?"

"Well, yes, if I understand, that is, correctly. Are you asking if I imagined sex with him now, here, or if I now and here was imagining sex with him?"

"Either one, Mr. uh, uh, either the sex now or whatever."

"Well, of course, I'm imagining all those things now, now that we're talking about it. I'm sure we're all imagining it now. Dexter and I, say, on this table, nude, the hot lights, some sort of furry rug . . . As I say, Doctor, all of us, sucking his sweet, hard . . . "

"Thank you."

"Here under the lights."

"It's quite enough."

"Slick with sweat."

"Yes, it's clear, quite clear."

"I find it hard to stop."

"You may insert your testimony at a later hearing, Mr. uh, uh, in a more private setting."

"I may?"

"When there's time. The Wellness Committee has a backlog to deliver."

"With a doctor?"

"If one is assigned."

"I must have one."

"If we so decide."

"To talk to. I still feel I misunderstand the guidelines."

---

*   *   *

I lay sleepless that first long night "home" in my new apartment. The empty walls echoed with murmurs and chair scrapes from my unseen neighbors. In the dark I tossed and shuddered like a caught fish. When dawn came I washed and dressed, eager for the morning rendezvous with my Doctor-General.

"Our goal is to help you organize your life in such a way that your deviant behaviors do not recur," he in fact began on our first morning, as promised. We sat facing one another in the heavy leather chairs of his outer chamber. "This involves more than simply punishment or isolation. We hope to redirect your desires and establish a structure to your life that will help you avoid temptation ... situations, and such. Certain occupational and social skills will be strengthened, while the various obsessive urges that have compelled you toward deviant action will be redirected. I'm talking about your love button. I rather see it as making whole what is now an incomplete person, helping you move past a stage of arrested growth."

I pardoned him the ugly language as I knew it to be part of his job. The vastness of his outer chamber allowed me an ease of breathing I had not felt before. Distinct from his therapeutic inner chamber (the site of our most intimate conversations) my doctor's expansive outer chamber projected a studied informality: an opened window or two, throw rugs dotting the floor like lesions, a ramshackle scattering of curios; sweet liqueurs, brightly colored, green, violet, and rose, sat radiant in their crystal decanters. The morning sunlight shone through them. I sat in a chair (rather too large) and felt like the child I once was, awaiting the merciless wisdom of the headmaster. He had his feet up on his desk, the scuffed leather soles presenting their faces to me. He'd still not told me anything about my new life.

"I see, Mr., uh, Doctor, but I'm still uncertain what it is I'll be doing each day."

"Each day? Each day will be different. This is not a program of incarceration, Mr. uh, uh, rather it is therapeutic in nature. You are free to come and go, to do as you see fit."

"'Mr. uh, uh?'" I asked, baffled by this queer form of address.

"Mr. uh, uh. Your name. The name you have been given to protect your anonymity."

"My name? But it's not a name at all."

"That's right. It's a hesitation, a failure to say a name. Solves the problem quite neatly, don't you think?"

"It certainly does, Doctor. Will the, uh, 'name' be permanent?"

"For the duration, Mr. uh, uh. You have certain protection during the course of your therapy. Certain rights."

"May I write to Dexter?"

"Oh, no, no. It's not the time for apologetic missives now. That time is long past. You'll have to give it a rest, my friend. Give yourself some distance from this . . . this obsession." Now he leaned toward me, and I could see the tiny creases in his skin. "It's time to begin asking yourself some questions." His teeth glistened and I felt a cloud of warm breath blow over me. "What exactly is it that you saw in him?"

"Him." Oh, yes. The word was like a powerful fume, and my head was awash with it, with "him," Dexter, and the vision of his delicate wrists, his heart beating visibly beneath his sternum, the shallow, perfect belly button, and the hollow of his collarbone where I would rest my tongue. Him. He was radiant, and this vision of him broadcast a simple, right answer to my Doctor-General's first alarming question: "Beauty," I spoke out loud. "What I saw in him was beauty." The doctor sat, baffled. "I am a lover of beauty . . . " Silence passed between us. He was motionless and warm. I have seen paintings of Christ which held this same stillness and affection. My head swam forward with its thought. "May I work with the children here?"

Strangely, he rose now as if to kiss me, stared, then he sat back down, recovering his usual aspect.

"Your new life will keep you clear of these temptations. No work with kids. No loitering near the school yards. Certain patterns must be broken if you are ever to move forward and seek self-esteem among adults."

"I'm to seek self-esteem among adults?"

"In a manner of speaking. Not actually setting out to search, rather, finding it there, as a matter of course, habitually, as it were."

"But what will I do all day?" I swung my legs over the leather arm of the easy chair. "What will I do each morning if I'm not going off to teach?"

"Your writing," he assured me, tipping slightly toward his desk. "Sessions, here, with me. And, of course, behavioral therapy."

"Alone?"

"With the technicians."

"Will my work . . . "

"Be alone? Yes. You have much reflecting to do."

On that, our first full day together in this the city of my new life, we went like a whirlwind from one stop to the next, the Doctor-General and myself. We rode the trams to and fro, across the busy districts north of the center, out to the parade ground on one occasion, and finally, at day's end, winding through the steep forested hills to the Vista. The freshness of the air was startling as the electric tram wound its way along the twin metal rails. The city seemed at a great remove, though it was easily visible through the trees to our west. The Doctor-General was gazing out across it, with his certain silent smile. There was so much that I had not mentioned to him, so many fears and questions, and yet I did not feel anxious. His strong shoulder bumped gently against me when the tram lurched forward. I glanced at his cheek, smooth and well-shaven, and felt the source of my calm. We were forever wed by his verdict. That thought, tracing through my mind as we sat then in the rattling car ascending higher into the evening, started a warmth inside me, a glowing below my heart, to which I would often return in times of confusion or doubt. I could look to him in silence or speech and find that communion, that mingling of purpose and situation, that I would so often need to reassure me: I had not been cast out or repudiated by the community that first taught me to love.

THE MORNINGS WERE DIFFICULT. MY APARTMENT, shadowed by taller buildings, sat but two stories up from the narrow street. Bells on the churches sang, and then dawn came with all its noise and transit. I might lie there in peace, half-sleeping, while umbrellas rustled below and the trams rang sharp warnings to crowds of hatted men. For a long moment I was snug, and guilty with the pleasure of my bed. Keys might jangle in a lock down the hall, or the muffled broadcast of a housewife's radio come seeping into my rooms . . . I would press my head to the pillow and sigh.

On typical mornings, such as the brisk and chilly one a few short weeks into this, my new life, my gaze would wander over the mottled folds of the duvet and come to rest on the awful black typing machine (with its idle keys). It bore a hole through my heart. I turned toward the wall and felt its pressure on my back.

According to the Doctor-General, as a writer I don't go to an office to work. I organize my hours around the spirit that has possessed me, answering to my muse. I've been provided with a manual typewriter and coffee mug, notepads and clean white sheets of paper, rumpled clothing, used furniture, and shelf loads of obscure, well-thumbed books. I miss the school terribly and wish to God the Ministry would restructure my new profession and construct enormous gray office flats to which every writer would report at nine A.M. on the dot. The open interior would be filled with row upon row of Formica desks and bulky electric typing machines. I'd set my lunch pail by my feet, grumble terse greetings to those writers nearest, and commence. Coffee break, an hour off for lunch at noon, and a fine clear steam whistle blowing at the stroke of five. I don't think the generals or the Ministry know what it's really like to write all day alone.

Oh, but I had just begun. My kind Doctor-General encouraged me at every turn. He saw my rocky start as evidence of high standards and commitment. "Painful comes the mother lode," he would say, and often.

At noon (that bright and typical day) I rose to the loud ringing of the bells and my street busy with workmen beginning their midday's meal. The clatter of the fish carts echoed along the lane and I knew that I'd missed the morning market again. Vendors loaded kale into burlap sacks. Others stacked sides of raw, smoked meat in boxes to be wheeled on dollies down the street to the harbor. The noise and bustle ought to have marked the end of my first session at the typing machine. Alas, I had slept in.

Leaning out the window, I sighed and took a breath of the new day's air. A flock of schoolkids wavered along the street on bicycles, off to lunch and, God knows, a cigarette or two. True to my promise, given solemnly to the doctor, I spoke not a word out the window to the passing boys.

It was a sparkling fall day, the sort on which the winds blow north, relieving the old district of the cursed ash and bringing a fresh, salty fish smell in from the harbor. These unpredictable gusts disturbed the otherwise pleasant air, taking hats from heads and blowing garbage up the face of my building. I would be meeting my Doctor-General this afternoon, to retrieve a small packet required for my session with the technicians). I prepared myself quickly and went.

The sun beat against the tram and warmed the tawdry vinyl seats. I looked across the valley of the gray factories, up into the billowing hills. The summer's green was still holding, touched here and there by the first turnings of fall. I had enjoyed a hazy nostalgia these first weeks back, finding lost lanes and bookstores I had known as a student. Vistas opened up, often, that I knew well in my heart, but which my mind had forgotten. This view east was one of these. The tram lurched past a billboard, obscuring the view, and I pulled the little bell meaning stop. The broad marble steps of the Ministry were just a half-block away.

The building's grand rotunda was almost empty. The Doctor-General always planned my visits for midday, or the evening—a slack time in any case—to make my travels easier. I found his door open and went in unannounced.

He was dressed in tweed, leaning thoughtfully over the wide mahogany desk. Sunlight poured in the windows and crossed through dusty air. A book lay opened before him, an edition of Egas Moniz, in the original Portuguese. A scholar to boot, my Doctor-General. He was motionless, lost in calculations, as if his body were put on hold so his mind could wander more freely.

"Ah, Mr. uh, uh," he sighed, looking up from the book. "Very prompt." He strode deliberately to the door and shut it, letting the lovely room enclose us completely. The silence of the mahogany settled like dust all around us. One could feel the weight of the building, the importance of the Ministry itself, in the unwavering line of his wood paneling. I admired the effect and opened my eyes wide to let the room's geometry extend itself inside my head.

"Tea, coffee?" he offered, gesturing to the pot of water by the fire. "It's quite fresh." Slight embers glowed among the fallen ashes. It had been a big fire and was now burned down. The night maid, I'm certain, built it in preparation for my Doctor-General's predawn arrival. It was part of his regimen.

We reclined upon the divan, stretched out by the fire, and shared tea, a small hospitality before the exchange of papers. In the outer chamber all was informality and light. The dim gaiety of the boulevard reached us through the windows, a distant sound. We drained our cups, chatting, and suffered a small vial of anisette. Pressured by the call of his important studies, my Doctor-General finished his liqueur in one swallow, handed me my packet (directions, pass, etc.), and sent me, instead, early to the laboratory of Flessinger and Ponz.

These technicians were a barbarous lot. They seemed to have been assigned to a life underground, sequestered like nuns or a jury. I approached the daunting façade of their "lair" with a quickened step, fearing the reproaches that were said to accompany a late arrival. The doctor's packet said so, amid frighteningly graphic instructions, and short dossiers (with photos) of the team assigned to my case. "Never be late," it warned in bold.

The wind beat upon the flags, buffeting them furiously. Applicants were gathered in bunches on the front steps, roped in by velvet and brass. I ducked under the steps, where the ministerial carriage was parked, and pulled the crocheted beckoning cord. It was Dilthy who answered, after peering at me through the spyglass for the customary fifteen seconds. "Afternoon, Dilthy," I said cheerfully, entering and removing my overcoat. "Ponz, Flessinger." They nodded, as one, but said nothing. "Fine day, eh?" A white gown was unfolded and I shed my garment. Ponz and Flessinger wrapped me in the gown and took me across the next threshold into their laboratory.

It was, in fact, a small room similar in style and ambiance to the Doctor-General's inner chamber. While somewhat larger than that "sanctorum," the laboratory of Flessinger and Ponz sported the same neutral wall tones and absence of an external portal, window, or door, as such. The room was empty, save for my chair and the projection screens. Flessinger sat me down and signaled to Ponz to ready the device. I opened the white gown (as per the instructions) and saw that my little friend was feeling quite shy, all snuggled up in his tangled nest. Ponz looked at me impatiently, not wanting to involve himself with my penis any more than was absolutely necessary.

I stared at him, and down at myself, feeling both innocent and somehow guilty. It was not clear to me exactly what state of arousal the technicians required. In the months that followed, despite twice-weekly sessions, it never became clear. If ever I arrived "in full flower" Ponz gave me a nasty, withering glance and stood tapping his toes impatiently, waiting for the crazy thing to calm itself down. It seems there was some median point at which attachment of the phallometer was easiest. Ponz would have no truck with anything else. He rolled his eyes at me and waited for the warmth of the room to have its encouraging effect.

Thankfully, the silly twosome left the room, always, following our ritual preliminaries. Once they'd secured the device and checked to see that I was accurately positioned, a hasty retreat would be beaten to the booth. There they began the calibrations. It was only then, through the intervention of a loudspeaker, that they would speak to me.

"Are you comfortable in your chair?" The voice was so tender and soft. I have no idea whether it was Flessinger or Ponz.

"Yes, quite comfortable."

"You may remove the gown now, if you wish." I did. The room contained a perfect stillness. The air passed in and out, through invisible ducts, caressing my skin like endless yards of silk.

"We're getting a reading, Mr. uh, uh. Is that confirmed?" the soft voice inquired.

"Uh-huh." I breathed, letting my shoulders and neck loosen. I had disturbed their calibrations; there was really no helping it. The first moments alone were invariably arousing . . . the muted tones, the circulation of the air, as I've said. Little glimpses of light, glimmering points of red and green, twinkling behind the black glass to my left. Sometimes a ghostly face would hover among them, bending close to a meter. When the films began the men became invisible.

"Let's find a plateau, if we can, please." I thought about history, as the Doctor-General's packet suggested, trying to sort out exactly how old the various signators were at the time of the first declaration. An impressionistic landscape painting appeared in front of me on the screen. "We'd like to get a calibration here if we could. Just focus on the slide, please."

A lovely meadow sat, dappled by the sun. The long, wet grass was painted a rich green, and the light seemed to indicate that it was early morning. You could see that, to the right, a small pond had collected with the spring rains. Lilac grew thick along its shore and the rippling waves of a boy's splashings could be seen in the disturbed face of the water. The fact that he was completely hidden from view seemed to suggest that he'd chosen to swim naked, perhaps with a special friend; the two of them, shy by nature, stayed out of the painter's line of sight. A marked stylistic break divided the painting top from bottom. Evidently the painter, a young woodsy man of twenty or twenty-five, full with life's vital sap, noting the boyish play of the little swimmers, took an extended break from his work to join them. Stripping his simple peasant garments off with a few strong tugs, he leaped with agility and grace into the spring-fed waters. The boys, naturally, seized upon him, trying their impish strength and wiles on and against his sturdy frame, wrapping their gangly limbs over him all hither and thither . . .

"I'm sorry, but we seem to be getting a reading. Could you focus on the slide, please?" I blushed warmly and pulled the gown up over my activity.

I had been told on day one the paintings were erotically neutral, simply calibration tools. But it was difficult to watch the slides—neutral or not—without looking in them for some point of interest. That this point of interest so often included a boy or two and some small degree of nudity was, I suppose, part of the reason I was here. I took several deep breaths and focused my attentions on the poorly rendered tree.

Our sessions were such a puzzle to me. I had imagined they would involve drugs or surgery, or training of the sort a circus bear might receive. It wasn't precisely racks and vices I had envisioned, hunks of meat tossed to prone men on cement floors, but it was something of that nature. The removal of the garments, for instance (as the first practice I encountered), did seem to presage radical methods, painful manipulations of the body or markings of the flesh. I never thought I would simply sit and watch dirty films, slouched in a comfy chair with my little friend dancing about in that warm, mysterious bag. There were, it's true, frequent and unpleasant interruptions, sudden eruptions of noxious gas, intermittent joltings from the arms of my chair. But I tried to ignore these, focusing, instead, on the images. I would imagine the intensity of my discomfort to be a sort of pleasure, as when Dexter grabbed and scratched at me so furiously when nearing orgasm. Pain, I have found, is an attribute of passion.

"If you're ready, Mr. uh, uh, we can proceed." It was the voice. Of course I was ready. I shifted my gown loose again, enjoying the dimming of the lights, and faced forward toward the screen. A few yards of black leader rushed by, specked and scarred by bright green scratches. The light flashed into my chamber and played over my skin. My eyes were adjusting quite quickly when a bright field of white burst open and the room was flooded. It was the cameraman's clumsiness, the soft back and bottom of an adolescent boy having achieved an arctic whiteness by inept manipulations of the shutter. The film wobbled into focus and fixed its frame; the white darkened down into an irresistibly Arabian skin tone as the cameraman, evidently, found his controls.

The boy lay back on a rug and turned onto his side, letting us gaze upon the entirety of his naked body. One could tell from the sparkle in his eyes, the cocky grin on his devilish face, that he was aware of his own beauty. He reached down across his smooth belly and took the limber length of his erect little friend in hand. Like the lively feet of a Labrador puppy, it was overly large and clumsy for the boy's slim frame. Its wet tip pushed up against his navel as he, still smiling with pleasure, played upon its length with his hand.

It was at this point, so soon into my viewing, that the mysterious joltings began (albeit at an intensity far below that which they sometimes reached). The sensations began in vaguely discernible points, but soon expanded like a pool of blood to warm me all over. They coursed across and through me in waves that must have been determined by the hands of Flessinger and Ponz, spinning their powerful dials. It took me aback for a moment, distracting my attention from the screen and onto my own body.

But the boy's delightful eyes beckoned me back; transfigured by his own pleasure, their depth and intensity increased in concert with my own electrical sensations. The shocks might have been coming from him, my body wired to his pleasure centers. Each increase in voltage seemed to be the product of his escalating passion. The film, Ponz and Flessinger, the chair: all of it was simply a mechanism through which he caressed me.

He was coming closer to orgasm, his legs spread out wider, his feet planted down and back arched. Yet still he looked at me, puzzled now, overcome; the muscular spasms of his body were repeated in his gaze. I, too, was nearly there, though I couldn't touch my penis, enclosed as it was in the instrument of my therapy. I felt myself mimicking his acrobatics. Noxious fumes filled the air, as if the indescribable stink of his pleasure had burst through the screen and engulfed me. I felt him penetrate me everywhere, electrical and primitive, awash in our mechanically multiplied effusions.

It became so much more than simply me and the boy or, rather, the image of the boy. Ponz and Flessinger, their mysterious booth and its apparatus, the Doctor-General and the Ministry that made it all possible ... I felt all of their attentions, their painstaking ministrations, fulfilled in that moment of coming; the very building and its edifice, the proud soldiers marching to the parade grounds. It all spun around my moment as an expression of love directed finally to me through those thin electrical wires that ran to my chair.

"Excuse me, uh, Mr.," the voice spoke. "The, uh, the panel indicates that you've fouled the mechanism." The film had trailed out as the boy lay back exhausted, come trailing in drops and pools from his brown chest down to his tummy. The screen went black again, and my chair was still and silent. Indeed, I had come in the cool, wired sack.

"I'm sorry."

With each session the accident would repeat itself. I soon became more baffled than sorry. Neither Ponz nor Flessinger volunteered any advice as to what I might do to avoid it in the future. I was afraid to breach the topic with the Doctor-General, fearing his judgment.

Ponz came out from the darkened booth pulling on his rubber gloves and casting disapproving glances. He removed the mechanism and cleaned me up before attaching a second one. This one would be spared any "fouling." I had not the sort of sexual stamina one reads about in the tabloids. The rest of the afternoon, typically, would be spent in a mild state of arousal, my little friend dipping and bobbing to the play of the images on screen. I sometimes found pleasure in the adults featured as counterpoint to the forbidden children, but the intensity of that interaction never matched what I felt for the boys, rarely, if ever, triggering the desired shocks and fumes.

Outside, the cool autumn night had descended over the city. The warmth was gone from the Ministry's stone steps. Trains rolled out of the crowded yards, shooting steam into the darkness. They let their warning bells ring as they left the city, going north and then east to the mountains. In front parlors children pulled on sweaters or coats to run into the night . . . to meet in secret their little friends for mischief . . . I walked alone, emptied by the puzzling intensity of my six hours in the chamber, and observed the cold stars in the night sky above. The tram rumbled past, but I made no move to beckon it. It rattled into the distance, light and warm, almost empty, making its way to the city center.

Among the distant noises of the harbor and the rustle of the banners, there among the sounds of the old district still a few blocks away, I thought I could hear a thin, small voice singing. It was "her" song, Lucrezia's song, though it was not Lucrezia who sang it. And it did not come from the houses, nor from the cafés, nor the plaza. The sound was borne in on the night air, as if from higher up, from above the city, perhaps from the dark hills to the east. I looked toward the Vista, in the moonless night, and searched among the faces of the wooded hills. Who was out there? And why Lucrezia's song?

Lucrezia. In my youth she towered over us, dominating the stage of the opera house. Six and a half feet tall in her bare feet (though no one had ever seen her in bare feet). She manhandled the stage under heels as tall and sharp as railroad spikes; her tiara clattered against the light pots, it seemed, lofted above on her fabulous curls. So much of what mattered most to me had been wrapped neatly around those halcyon days of Lucrezia's vibrance and glory, those long months of her triumph upon the opera house stage.

There was a moment then, in that long ago past, an extended moment of perfection, when all was right with the capital and countryside, before the banners began their rapid, almost weekly, changes, when the citizens seemed to walk with their eyes wide and sensitive to the ocean air, the liveliness of the streets, the importance, palpable as a humming, of each busy table in the cafés where we'd sit and drink chocolates. All that was best in us thrived in lively exchanges of opinion and song, in the spontaneous expostulations of radicals or schoolboys, anyone with legs strong enough to climb up on the tabletop. Our vitality achieved its pinnacle in Lucrezia, in her triumph on the stage. Each day the capital was abuzz with anticipation. Every café filled with revelers on their way to stand near to the opera house and catch any trace of sound that might drift out. It was the childhood of our city. And she was our voice and soul, the embodiment of an insatiable vitality that, by some accident of history, our culture stumbled upon for its brief, shining moment.

But those days passed. Policies changed; the opera house was stripped of artifice and became a stage for therapeutic dramas. She was taken from her dressing room one night, they say, robbed of her costume, and left to starve on the street. Her song was banned, and she found her way to the Burlesque, where she is kept like an animal, a trained circus freak, in a basement off the

Fish Street. Seven shows a week she sings now, every night until dawn. On some nights I go there (top secret, for fear of my D.G.N.N.) and I join the lusty voices joining hers.

Who could be singing her song now, under cover of dark? And where? Enchanted by the whispering contralto, I stopped still and redoubled my inspection of the hills.

There *was* something, up above the reach of the tram line, on the crest running north from the Vista. A dim glow of light from a campfire. It flickered behind the trees, dancing yellow and orange in the night. In its light I could see two large banners, unfurled and rustling in the wind: strange, unfamiliar banners with no insignia, at least none that I could recognize from this distance. The song carried down to us from that encampment, from on high, as it were. In the stillness of the plazas, among the deserted buildings of the ministries, it could be heard clearly.

The peace was shattered by two monstrous scrub trucks lurching from the portals of their electronically shuttered garages and sashaying onto the Criminal and Health Plaza. Litter and dust flew in their wake (until the hoses came on). I hurried away toward the old district, with the trace of her melody inhabiting my mind.

The next morning came, bright and cold, a harbinger of the fall that would, in turn, usher in winter. I opened my windows to the brisk air, letting it wash the sleep away. It billowed and cleared my stuffy room of dust and sloth.

Below, the lobster man (as I called my elderly neighbor) emerged from our doorway and, looking up, beckoned to me with a crooked finger. I was to join him for lunch at the small bistro on our busy corner. It was a remarkable fact that my mysterious neighbor required, at most, two hours' sleep each night. I might see him just returning from the Burlesque (he shared my fascina-

tion with Lucrezia) or, fresh as a flower, leaving again for breakfast, and all within the first hours of morning.

We walked the long blocks arm in arm, as is the custom
among older gentlemen. The lobster man's face was an unreadable mass of folded, scabbing flesh. His natural hair flopped atop
this baffling head. As we ambled down the street he gave no
ground to pedestrians coming toward us. The lobster man
asserted de facto the privileges of age and decrepitude, and
barked curses at all who looked askance.

"And how is your *oeuvre?*" he inquired coolly as we settled in
at our small table. My "oeuvre," truth be told, was a source of
great anxiety for me. The lobster man dragged a breath of smoke
from his messy cigarette and let it drift back out again, enveloping his face like a shroud. Wine was served. I said nothing,
embarrassed by my failure. In fact, I had only produced a few
slim pages.

"I don't see you offering pages to be read, bouncing ideas off
me as you said you would." He stuck his nose deep into the
largely crimson wineglass, waves of the heady liquid tickling his
nostrils. Still his eyes kept on me, requesting an answer. I blushed
and shrank just a little in my chair.

"Well . . . the writer's life!" I raised my eyebrows suggestively.
"Fascinating, really. Different every day. I have half a mind to
write a book about it."

"It's all so very new to you, I'm sure. I had trouble too," he
confided, "when I was first assigned."

"You were a writer?"

"Theater, books, the occasional introduction."

It had never occurred to me. I had simply presumed (in the
few weeks I'd known him) that he was with the university. Perhaps
it was his look, the indecipherable lumpiness of him, which was to
some degree replicated by the professors. The tenderness of his

confession drew his eyes downward. He cast glances from shoe to shoe.

"Before the new discoveries?" I asked thoughtfully. I couldn't imagine the lobster man having anything to do with the new theater, caustic and old-fashioned as he was.

"Oh yes, yes. Long before any of that." He leaned across the table to me, his lips wet with the hearty wine. "I wrote for Lucrezia, when she first began." The lobster man filled my glass, watching my eyes, aswim with memories. "You knew of her then?" he asked.

"Yes," I said softly, drinking the wine to warm me. "I saw her first when I was nineteen. *Cleopatra in Winter*."

"Yes, yes. In March, a year and a half before her removal. I was there."

"Inside?"

"Oh yes, I was always let in, being a writer for her."

"I'd been outside several times before I was able to find a way in."

"Hmm," the old man sighed. "One of the many, the throngs of boys clamoring outside. I remember well."

"I suspect I saw you arriving."

"Oh no, no. I think not. I was quite discreet. I wasn't among those in the fancy carriages with all their foofarol."

"I made her a costume once." This brought a shift in the lobster man's posture (as I had hoped it would).

"One she used?"

"Yes. A carapace. She was carried off in it at the closing of the last show."

"*Agonies of a Fly?*"

"Yes, the last week."

"But of course I saw it. I, I wept. The vaulting fans, they, they tickled the upper reaches of the light bank."

"Yes."

"And they shimmered so, the way she'd wag her head as if it were nothing."

"Neck strong as an ox they say."

"And correctly. She's not one to get in a bullybout with. It was a beautiful costume."

Time passed. The crowd thinned considerably, and the bottle was drained. The lobster man leaned toward me and whispered "Five P.M., come to my apartment. I have something that might interest you." He put his finger to his lips meaning "hush-hush" and then fell asleep. The waiter brought a small pillow to comfort him. I took my hot chocolate in slow sips and wondered about his secret. How like a child he seemed, lost in dreams.

I folded my napkin and left. The lobster man slumped, ajar in his cane chair, watched by the solicitous waiters. The sky was a deep azure blue (cleansed by the violent rains that came at night), and I went off to my errands. By five I was home and knocking on my crustaceous neighbor's door, 2A.

He answered with terse grumbles, dressed in his robe and slippers, with reading glasses slipping down his nose. I'd brought my tea with me, and held two biscuits clutched tightly to my mug.

In the curtained room, photographs of pugilists obscured the walls. Yellowed portraits hung haphazardly, crowding up against each other. They were dim in the shadows.

"My hobby," the lobster man explained. "My oldest brother was a pugilist." He pointed to one photo, much smaller than the others. "He wasn't very successful in the ring." He paused to find exactly the words for what he was thinking. "But he did gain a certain purity from it."

I looked at the photo, searching the face and posture for this "purity." Trapped in gray anonymous light, he stood before a cheap painted backdrop of the boxing ring where he practiced his art. The strong white chest seemed to invite the surgeon's knife, firm and still, like the ample, bloodless chest of a cadaver. The brother simply stared past me, his arms raised and motionless. I was reminded of the Prime Minister, just then, and his astonishing gaze. It danced around the room gaily like a butterfly, alighting upon each camera in turn with the rhythm and speed of a cocktail party hostess. The remarkable result of this inspired performance was the feeling that one had been paid special attention, though deftly and with tact. The pugilist had none of this. He seemed blind to all society.

"You see, they had no concerns except to fight well. Their bodies were meant simply to fight, to hit cleanly and to withstand the blows of the opponent."

"Were you yourself a pugilist?" I asked, fiddling with his papers. The discussion had begun to make me nervous, seeming to border as it did on ideology or politics. The tea in my mug was cooling. The lobster man's silence provoked me from my place and I began a small flurry of cleaning. I flitted across the room, picking up old mugs and full ashtrays, transporting them to the kitchen and its overfull washbasin.

"Do you mind?" I called out, indicating the drape cord. I gave it a fierce tug and the drapes flew back along their tracks, letting off small clouds of dust as they went. The bright afternoon was startling. My name seemed to be written on several sheets of paper laid out on the floor. There was, at the top of each, the word "SALON," capitalized as I have here written it.

"Tell me about the 'Salon.'" He disappeared into the bathroom, where a small kettle was plugged into the wall.

"Oh my, yes." He chuckled. He watched me while pouring boiling water into a teapot. "It is the reason I invited you over. The little something I had for you to see."

"Has it to do, then, with the 'hush-hush'?" He nodded his head eagerly.

"Yes, yes. Precisely. It's a small concern run by . . . well, we'll call him 'Doctor Cotton,' catering primarily to the ministers. You'll find it's all very fancy, and really quite rewarding." He sat down beside me on the soft bed. "Naturally I thought of you when you told me you were responsible for that astonishing carapace Lucrezia wore in her final appearance." I accepted the tea.

"Is it, I mean, *the* Salon?"

"*The* Salon? I'm really not at liberty. I mean, it is the best, the very best in face-lifts and prosthetics, offered only to the ministers and a handful of other dignitaries. And they need a new man to work in makeup and reconstruction."

The very thought made my head spin. The Salon was the last bastion of the grand stage. The ministers with their carefully maintained faces, their identities (so central to the smooth functioning of our city), went there to be crafted and refined by the makeup men. It was indeed hush-hush—a secret kept by everyone. To see its doors opening now to me made the blood rush to my face.

"A new man?" I whispered, not yet believing.

"A new man."

"Is there any . . . deception involved?" I asked.

"Well, yes. Yes there is, certainly."

"I mean on my part. Is my participation hush-hush?"

"Your identity will be kept from everyone involved."

"Yes," I then whispered. "Yes, I will do it."

"You'll do it?" My haste surprised him. "You'll not start until Monday, I'm afraid."

"Yes."

"And you must remember, hush-hush."

"Oh, yes."

"I'll make the arrangements." He offered me a sheaf of papers. There was a hand-drawn map atop the little pile. "It's quite near, behind the opera house." I studied the dim, scrawled map, observing the whimsical names listed at its bottom.

"Who are these people?" I asked, pointing toward the names.

"Doctor Cotton is in charge. You will ask for him when you get there. The others are co-workers, pseudonymous, of course. You are 'Mr. Sludge,' or will be so known by the men at the Salon."

"'Mr. Sludge'?"

"To preserve your anonymity."

I WAS NERVOUS ON THE EVE OF MY FIRST DAY AT THE SALON. I
passed the hours with possible outfits, trying to create (from the
paucity of garments afforded a writer) something secretly flam-
boyant. The green carnation was unusable, its specificity long
since lost to sloppy usage. I tried my writer's tweed, buttoning all
three buttons, and fashioned a pastel tie around my vaulting collar. This was getting close. With a simple folding-down of the collar and the undoing of the buttons I appeared to be a student or,
perhaps, a professor, a member, in any case, of the academic community and its rumpled, amorphous fashion system. But with the
buttons fastened and the collar turned up, I was verging on the
look of a dandy.

This would do very well. I set the garments out for the morning and climbed into bed.

My room was silent and dark and I lay, still awake, looking at
the pale white form of my next-day's clothing. The street was
quiet now. Looking above me into the dark I saw cracks in the
plaster. It had been laid on thin and was eaten away by moisture.
A wave of drowsiness, like nausea, pulled the ceiling apart further.
I was tired, certainly, but something about the recent turns my

life had taken gave my exhaustion a panicked edge. The lattice of wood seemed to actually press down on me. Was there some sort of insect that had devoured the plaster? Or was it just the flimsiness of the building's construction . . . I pried at it with my eyes, and felt my bed sink beneath me. I wished for sleep to come on completely, and ease my mind. And then a peculiar thing happened. My body fell back too, and I rose, passing through the plaster and the ceiling above me. I moved swiftly into the air, spread cold as ice over chimneys and bell towers, until, like a fabric, I covered the city and the hills; a bracing wind, a night sky pocked with stars. I lay still abed and I mingled above us, my eyes clear and cold. I drifted over air blown from the sea, beyond the reach of machines and birds. What was it that took me then? I dropped near and wide, my throat tasting the wintry sky. I was the city and the hills to the east. What ubiquity, my position! I was an ocean, an ice floe, an empty place, and not a place at all. I was spread out, sparkling with colored lights above thin metal tracks running north and then east.

What hovered above those hills? What presence hung like breath in air? I was contained, suspended and dispersed, a cousin to the factory's ash. A fire burned in the woods, illuminating banners. Men sat on stones left by ice withdrawn long ago, breathing the same air as that which the Ministry found trapped in bubbles under the Arctic cap.

To remain there, in that thought, I might turn my eyes to the soft clothing I'd laid out in my room. I might glance at the apartment of the lobster man as he readied himself for the Burlesque, or the empty chambers of the Doctor-General, their darkness a perfect costume for my body.

But only to glance, to resurrect the center of my perception by skirting around its edge. Something lay waiting, something uncostumed and ignorant of time. Was it in the hills or beyond them?

A presence lay waiting, exceeding me, involving me. A presence? A past? I was enmeshed in it and not as action, movement, or change. It had always been so. Where it had gone, or not gone, been relegated to, it had gone evasively, pushed away by our nervous distractions ... bright smiles and noisy marching bands, impressive buildings and new leaders, the colorful fashions of the new season. And that presence, that past, was lost in the spectacle. Yet it remained with us, mingling in the sulfurous air, clattering along the metal rails.

Had the boys from the technical school noticed, sneaking out into the courtyard to escape the watchful eyes of the housemaster? Were the ministers aware, scribbling last notes at their midnight desks before warm milk and a fitful sleep? Would I remember or ever know what I, that evening, abed, felt? All that was left was the trace of a dream ... Dexter, with his wet perspiring chest, and the run of my tongue down across his ribs to his belly button. Dexter pushing my head down farther still, dancing his eager little friend against my face and lips, laughing, as he did, with the simple delight of it. I pushed my face onto the cool side of my pillow and listened to the lobster man disappear down the hall. He was going, as he did every night, to the Burlesque. My mind made its way strenuously toward sleep.

When I woke up it was dawn. The heavy wooden wheels of the vendors' carts could be heard turning, clacking and groaning against the cobblestones. The milk was being brought in, and the first editions of the morning newspaper sat in stacks by the kiosks. The sky was gray and unremarkable, as it sometimes is before a heavy snow. The air tasted of metal or coal. There was a holiday emptiness on the streets, as if everyone had gone away, leaving only transients to people the public squares. I turned my coat collar up as I left the apartment building. It was pleasant, really, to find the city so deserted. I walked toward the flat valley of the gray factories, just north, on the eastern edge of the ministries.

I do not understand the factories. Their tall metal stacks rise up into the sky alongside the broken remains of the structures they've replaced. The fallen ruins spread out in small pools around the factory grounds. The blackened bricks of the old smokestacks still rise, cresting like freakish waves in broad circles eight or ten yards high; then they collapse in on themselves. The weight of their years dragged them down from inside. Now they form barren cisterns, their enclosures filled by the rains. Nothing grows here. The rains gather and freeze in winter. The water leaks out or spills over the top. No one swims in the ruins, not even children in search of danger or fun.

As a boy I had several friends whose fathers and mothers worked in the factories. The closest was Herman, a boy one year older than I, who lived here in the houses of the first hill. We had been together since the primary school, adjacent by virtue of our last names, but never had a friendship until our first years in secondary. It was then, when I was thirteen, that I came to visit Herman at his house and first saw the valley in all its nearness and detail.

My family lived north of the city in a wealthy enclave of large houses scattered over the wooded hillsides. My father's work with the university brought him into town each day, but I rarely came with him, never, in fact, until I was eleven or twelve. All those years of my childhood were spent in the sheltered emptiness of our neighborhood or with my mother, going to the library where she volunteered. I spent many afternoons on my bicycle, clattering along with cards pushed into the spokes, riding imaginary races through the quiet woods and along the empty streets.

My father went on Saturdays to the old district in the city center, to search through secondhand bookshops, always going alone and returning late in the evening with talk of the day's events and, to my delight, small caricature drawings of the people he had seen along the way. These were hastily penned sketches done on the sly in a little notebook he always kept with him. He had no artistic ambition to speak of, and not much talent, but he was a sharp caricaturist. Several times, when I was older, I was sure that some old man or woman was exactly the one I'd seen drawn by my father years before. It may have been so, but I never knew. Father stopped making his caricatures when I was twelve and never let me have or see the old books after that.

It was that year (when I was twelve) that I began going down to the old district, alone, each day after school. Unable to articulate any reason more honest or compelling, I told myself that I was looking for books, rare books that could only be found in the secondhand shops. I had no interest at all in reading these books. To actually have them would have destroyed their usefulness. It was the *lack* of them that I found useful and that I desired. I did not tell my mother or father about these trips, lying to them instead about a sports team I said I'd joined. At some level I knew they must never find out about my journeys into town.

When my friendship with Herman began the next year, it was only natural that I enlist him in my secret practice. This was an event of the greatest importance to me, an acknowledgment of something intimate and monumental (though I had no idea what exactly that was). Unbeknownst to Herman, for several months I kept a meticulous account of his actions, evaluating his worthiness and the possibility and timing of my invitation.

Herman was a small boy, not as strong or physical as I was, but certainly as lonely. He shared with me that most important quality, solitude—a characteristic that runs only in a few children and binds them more tightly one to another than any other force. I initiated our friendship by asking him for help I did not need on some history reading. Looking back I can see what compelled me toward him—the strangeness and power of this new world (the one in which I sneaked away from my family's home to explore the city's center) demanded a companion, someone also new to it.

That companion was Herman, I guess, simply because I *saw* him one day. I saw him and noticed something in his eyes, the carriage of his neck and shoulders. The tram threw us together, actually, one afternoon as our class went to the public swimming pool. It turned sharply and all of us who were standing were tossed into one another, I against him. It was remarkable, as if I'd never before actually known that he was a living thing. The way his little body gave against my weight, and then his hand pushing on my chest to help me back up again. He had always been nothing to me, equivalent to the school desks I saw each day. Now I looked at his blushing cheeks and at his eyes (which were nearly as black as his thick hair) and I recognized him. I saw, I guess, beauty in him. The rest of the way there I let my arm lie on his shoulders (and not unself-consciously) to steady myself. And I began wondering what it was I could say to extend this feeling. I decided finally upon my request that he visit my house and help me with some reading.

Herman and I became fast friends. We invariably went to my house or with my family when we did things together. He would stay with me through the dark winter afternoons, sometimes taking dinner with my family, and he'd return home by the trams, never asking me to join him and never accepting the rides offered by my parents. On weekends he'd stay over, the two of us sharing my narrow bed high up in the attic where I'd made my room. It was a badge of my independence. I insisted on moving all my belongings up there where I would not be disturbed by the noise of my parents' parties. Now that I was old enough, they had the good sense to go away most weekends, off on train trips and visits to other cities. Herman and I roamed the huge empty house like renegades, not bothering to change out of our nightshirts until Sunday evenings, when my parents would return.

I took him, finally, with me on the weekend of my fourteenth birthday. We met by the trams and rode all the way to the central square under the breaking rains of a spring storm. Do I remember this correctly? There was the factory, seen from the rattling tram, flashing in and out of sight between the buildings. It was, then, still the old brick factory. Dark ash rolled out of the stacks into the violent storm. In the dirty buildings where the workers sat, innumerable machines clattered, hidden behind the filthy glass windows. Beneath the storm their light was warm and welcoming, as if it came from the windows of some small cottage on a rain-drenched heath.

I didn't know that Herman's parents worked there, nor that he imagined only that he would finish school and go on to take his place there as well. It was not a bad place. The workers received a good wage and worked in conditions if not of comfort, then at least of safety. But from the tram that day, catching glimpses of it from between the intervening buildings, it looked like some despised cousin, a monstrous relative maimed or disfigured at birth and kept in a back room.

We started staying at his house as often as at mine. We'd walk back along the first hill and down the empty street toward the factories. The stacks loomed above us, their sooty air drifting over the hills. All the houses looked so similar and sad to me, jarring in their difference from what I had imagined the city held. It's not that I thought any less of my friend. (In fact, I invested Herman with an allure, based simply on his relation to the valley of the gray factories.) All of our time was spent together now, wandering the dusky lanes of the old district, spending the nights together at his house or holed up in my attic room, lying there in the warm bed talking.

Herman moved away that summer after our exams. We had

planned a train trip to the east, an adventure to celebrate our passing, but he and his family had gone even before our marks were posted. He had said nothing about their going, evidently not knowing how to say it, and simply sent me a card from the new city to which they had moved. I never wrote back.

It makes me bitter recalling this, but that was not the point of my story. All of it was simply to say, as preface, what it is I feel when I see the factory and why it is, perhaps, I am unable to understand its place and position. Looking, for instance, at the crumbled ruins of the old brick chimneys, their still pools of black water reflecting the sky that morning, I might have felt more than I could adequately say.

I stayed only a short time by the factory gates before turning away to catch a tram. The presence behind me of the long, flat valley reminded me of my last-night's revel . . . floating above it all. That valley and all it contained was elusive, too, and irrefutable. The factories' work went on, no matter how far away the tram took me. But there was little more I could do with that thought, and like my night's dream, it drifted away from me.

The door of the Salon was discreetly marked with a plastic coat of arms announcing a fanciful university, *Mutatis Universitas*. I pressed the small button protruding from the stone wall and heard a hasty shuffling from within.

"Yes?" a man's wary voice asked.

"Doctor Cotton?" I asked, ignorant of any codes that might have been conventional.

"What exactly do you mean?" The door jiggled back at me.

"Are you Doctor Cotton?"

There was a long silence. My inquisitor walked away. I had hoped that things would be more aboveboard. In my fantasy the Salon had bright windows with lace curtains pulled back. Patrons sat in chrome and leather chairs (like the barber has) and a little bell would tinkle with the frequent opening and closing of the front door. Heavy footsteps drew close to the actual and unyielding portal.

"Mr. Sludge?" a new, friendlier voice asked.

"Yes," I replied, "I am Mr. Sludge."

"You should've said that to begin with." Several latches were disengaged and the heavy door swung open.

The interior was quite cheery, sporting floral pastel wallpaper and portrait photos hung in even rows along a narrow hallway. The hallway led to a brightly lit room filled with just such chairs as I had imagined in my fantasy. But no windows opened up here. The only vistas were photographic. A hillside of fall birches, for example, spread across the anterior wall of the common workroom, enclosed in *trompe l'oeil* window frames of burnished oak. An alpine vista opened up to the left. The photo sported rough fir shutters, ajar, cruelly inviting the absent spring air to blow through them. Cows stood stock-still all along the green hillsides, one gazing in at us from a short distance away.

Doctor Cotton led me quickly through to his office, a charmless beige cubicle with tables and a small array of office machinery. We sat down at the large vinyl-covered desk.

"Welcome, Mr. Sludge, this is it. Twelve chairs, twelve men on, four A.M. to midnight. You'll be working daytimes."

"Twelve men? How elaborate."

"Strictly business, Mr. Sludge. We have a job to do and, by God, we do it. No questions asked."

"Certainly," I offered unsurely. "Or certainly not."

"Same chair every day; you've brought your kit?"

I hadn't. I looked at and around the "doctor," checking the neat piles of paper, the chromatically arranged putty samples. I knew there was no use evading. "I left it at home."

"Not to worry. It's still day one."

"Thank you, sir."

"We'll just begin with the overview and general procedures, give you the tour, and let you get your kit at lunchtime. There might be a little work for you this afternoon."

Where had he met my lobster man? They seemed worlds apart in manner and tact. Probably they'd known each other through the stage, Lucrezia and all that. Anyone could be a fancier of Lucrezia. There really were no outward traits that marked us. At the doors of the Burlesque each night, the most puzzling motley of men gathered. Husbands of the factory, their patched windbreakers zipped up tight against their throats, withered academics feigning interest in some obscure chapbook, chefs and waiters, boys from the outlying districts, policemen whom you might see the next day and smile inwardly at the fact of your shared enthusiasm.

And *these* priviliged men of the Salon had met long before all of that, when Lucrezia played at the opera house. I recognized an old face or two, men I'd seen almost a decade past, polishing up their tools during the morning break. What peculiar good fortune that my most passionate work of those distant days, helping to create the triumphant artifice of Lucrezia, had caught the eyes of their comrade and led me now to the threshold of this grand opportunity. Doctor Cotton escorted me back through the short maze of parlors and passageways, pointing out the functions and fixtures in each room, including the Chamber of Totality as he called it, a tiny black room crowded with gleaming chrome instruments and one engulfing leather chair, hydraulically manipulated and festooned with straps.

"We handle most emergencies here," he told me in a hushed whisper. "Major facials, the more complicated prosthetics." The warm black leather beckoned, coffinlike, calling me to rest upon it. It reminded me of my own chair in the laboratory of Flessinger and Ponz. The leather was of the same ministerial stock, the padding as ample and artfully arranged.

"May I," I asked timidly, "sit for a moment?" Doctor Cotton fidgeted, squinching his face.

"But why on earth?" he asked, putting me off.

"Just briefly, to rest."

Doctor Cotton turned and walked down the hall, like a wise mother leaving her young son to pee in the men's room. I let the heavy door close behind him, shutting out the hall's light. The chamber's warmth and stillness enveloped me, offering nothing for my eyes. The heavy steel table bumped my shin and rolled a few inches forward. I could taste the chair, my mouth and nose open just so, my breath drawn slowly through. It was salty sweet in the lightless room. I moved forward and felt it there against me, the resplendent leather giving a pressure like Dexter's insatiable hands. It could plausibly be him, his bottom perhaps, pushing against my thighs. I imagined it so and climbed on top, splaying my body across this receptive partner; then I let my buckle loose to allow a degree of intimacy.

What fantastic lines this chair had, fitted like a glove to my body. Its center point had a narrowness, a sudden slimming as with Dexter when I ran my hands down his ribs and reached that point above his hips where I would squeeze him. I wrapped my arms around this spot vigorously, clasping my two hands together behind the chair. This created greater leverage and allowed me to perform a cluster of amorous thrustings, my engorged little friend snuffling and burrowing among the folds of padded leather. Was it Dexter I was imagining, supine beneath me? Dexter was never so passive. His lithe body and frisky limbs were as a whirlwind, all hither and thither. Every moment surprised me, never knowing where I'd find him next, in what acrobatic relation to my own groping arms.

If it was him (and, despite anything I may say, it certainly was) it was also and equally the chair of Flessinger and Ponz. In this my new life I had no erotic association to rival the excitement of their chair. I could not see. I pressed my face into the leather, smelling a hodgepodge of my erotic past. The lights came blindingly on and I could barely make out the impatient face of Doctor Cotton standing in the open doorway. He sported a mixture of surprise and fright, like that of a man on a precipice. His mouth had dropped open, but he shut it resolutely, closed the door, and knocked as if having just arrived.

"Mr. Sludge," he called tentatively. "Are we almost ready to proceed?" The bright lights insisted this was not so, that Doctor Cotton had indeed *been* inside, not outside, and that he knew very well I was still indisposed. I tucked my little friend back into his area and pulled my buckle shut. The bright gleam of the steel table offered a makeshift mirror. I checked my appearance, smoothed my wrinkled clothing, and rearranged my hair. In the hallway Doctor Cotton wiggled his eyebrows and said nothing. He called me to his office with a wave of the hand.

A contract was placed neatly on his desk. It contained more clauses than I could possibly read, and a long black line on which I was to sign.

"Before we proceed, Mr. Sludge, let me say one thing and then let the subject be dropped." He paused. "Be aware that we in the Salon are accustomed to eccentricity. It is part of our daily work and we will not condemn it in any man. But we are accustomed, as well, to a great degree of discretion and tact. I hope my meaning is clear. Please sign here." He pointed his fountain pen toward the empty black line.

"What does it say?" I asked.

"It is a vow, a pledge to submit urine should the need arise."

"And that's all?"

"No, there are other clauses. A loyalty pledge assuring the Salon of your intentions and your commitment to discretion and secrecy."

"Yes, and?"

"An admission of guilt, to be used against you in case of emergency. Standard contractual language. Nothing really, sign, please."

"Guilt about what?"

"Not guilt *about* something, Mr. Sludge. This is not a therapeutic confessional. It's general culpability for any crimes that should come to the attention of the Parks Rangers."

"Any crimes?"

"Well, actually it's just a blank space. We fill it in later, if there's a need."

"What need?"

"In case of scandal or discovery if the Salon should come to the attention of the public or factions that might disapprove. We can't have the whole institution come tumbling down. Your admission of guilt helps pave the way for a less upsetting solution."

"I've never seen a contract like this before."

"You've never worked at the Salon. It's a great privilege."

"Yes, yes, I know. I'm honored, really, and eager to begin. But why must I submit urine or whatever?"

"The clause merely affirms your willingness to surrender your urine, 'should the need arise.'"

"I see."

"Not to worry, no one's ever been asked. Just your name, right there on the black line."

"My real name?"

"Don't be silly, of course not. Why, I'd no idea you even *had* a real name. 'Sludge' will do, 'Mr. Sludge.'"

I took the slim blue fountain pen and wet its nib on my tongue. A contract signed "Mr. Sludge" should be safe enough, having no claim on my real new life (as it existed outside the ruse of my work at the Salon). I put pen to paper and scripted the unfamiliar name floridly. It looked rather nice, so brief and to the point. "Mr. Sludge." No first name, as none had been assigned. Doctor Cotton seemed pleased. He snapped the contract up and slipped it into a slim cardboard envelope.

One can have a personality so easily, as it only requires a few distinctive features, a desire or two, a nervous habit. An empty life can be made full with a day's work, researching, to begin, the wide variety of personalities available (and their composition) and then constructing the rudimentary parts (whether prosthetic or behavioral). But my Doctor-General had designed a more prolonged and labored approach for me in this my new life. It was one of the terrible mysteries. Why and for how long?

Exactly that question occurred to me as I sat, illumined by the dappling A.M. sunlight near the tall windows of the Doctor-General's outer chamber. The ground was hard and the fields thick with frost. My footfall had crunched as if on shattered glass, walking the long boulevard to our early morning therapy. Even September can bring a killing frost. The ground stays hard until midday, when the sun finally warms it. The Doctor-General, who had spent the night immersed within his own researches (right here in this very room), had a fire set blazing by the hearth and a pot of strong coffee to warm me.

"The prospect, my friend, of such methods is what keeps me here unaware of the passing hours." He took the pot of coffee from the fire and pointed at his midnight labors. "It's outside the realm of current methods and so I'm not free to devote regular hours to its pursuit." A small, unconscious mouse was strapped to the desk, its tiny head cut open to reveal a gray lump of pudding which I took to be its brain.

The Doctor-General was well aware of my impatience with the "talking cure" and shared, I believe, some of my misgivings. He had "a hunch," he called it, about surgical manipulations of the mind. "I am still years away from any level of proficiency. And that is simply for work on mice. I doubt I'll ever develop the skills without the Ministry freeing me up to devote full time to it."

So often my therapy involved a working out of *his* concerns. But I did not resent it. In fact I felt rather special, privy as I was to his most intimate secrets. It was, perhaps, his way of establishing a model for my erection of meaningful adult relationships. I sank further into my soft leather chair. The comfort of his outer chamber had seduced me (as it always did) into a feeling of ease and belonging. It was my Doctor-General's one-two punch, the preliminary dawdlings in the outer chamber, a seemingly endless bliss followed at some moment of total surprise with a sudden call to the severity of the inner chamber.

He rose, unspeaking, and walked past me. The panel slid clear and he opened the door. It was silent, the small chamber clean. My couch was unruffled, its coverlet neatly tucked in just as it always was. I put the bag on my head and lay down, shifting on the cushions to settle myself. I heard his pen touch paper, and then nothing. The bag's muted light, so bleak after the dappling of the morning sun, steeled me.

There was a moment, as if between heartbeats.

"Are you perfectly comfortable?" he asked, disembodied. The words floated in air only long enough to be heard. "Is your bag too tight?"

"No, I feel quite fine. The bag fits me." His manner was so gentle, tender as a little boy's tongue.

"Your arms are relaxed? Your neck loose?" He brought calm to each part merely by the careful recitation of their names. "Legs settled, your muscles languid and calm?"

"Yes they are, thank you. Have you put your bag on?"

"Yes I have." He was always prompt, ready without rushing or fumbling as I sometimes did. My asking was simply a habit. We sat for a few unmarked moments.

"What are you thinking now?"

"The bareness of the trees, yesterday afternoon, when I was looking out the café window. Some maples still held on to their leaves. But they'll be bare within a few days."

Leaves dropped like water, slipping loose with each breath. I couldn't see them because of my mask, though I felt them parting from me, shivering off my skin, leaving me bare upon the couch.

"What about the bare trees?"

"They're very strong, to stay that way through winter." There was a tall maple in our front yard when I was young. It was bigger than the house, or seemed so to me. Each winter when the heavy storms came it would take the burden of snow onto its limbs. Everything would be muffled and silent, when suddenly an awful sharp crack would be heard, as if from a basement chamber of horrors, and some huge part of the maple would come crashing down to the ground in a flurry and would lie there while the weather buried it. It went on like this for years, until one hard winter it was reduced to nothing and my father cut it up for firewood.

"What are you thinking of now? The trees?"

"They cover the hillsides. I'd like to see them sometime, from above, all the hills and the mountains to the east. They covered the city, too, the hills where the city is. Can you imagine? When I go to the Vista, sometimes I'll walk in the woods. There's a small clearing to the north where you can look out at the ocean and see only the park land and the trees, as if the city wasn't there."

"Do you go there often?"

"Once in a while, if I have the afternoon free and want to get away from things."

"Get away from what sort of things?"

"Other people mostly, all the clamoring."

"Why?"

"To get some distance. I'd never think to live outside a city. I mean, isolated somewhere like a hermit. I couldn't bear it. I just need to keep things at a distance, get a proper view."

"Yes, I understand."

"Could we, sometime, go up in a balloon, above the city, and see the whole of it from above? Just once?"

"What do you imagine it would be like?"

"Oh, from above? Spectacular, all of it laid out there beneath us, visible in all directions, can you imagine? Some things I'll never understand. To see the hills and the city and the sea, all as one, all in their place. I can't tell you what it would mean."

"Have you always wanted to see the city from above?"

I supposed I had, though it had never taken on the immediacy it had in recent weeks. "I've never felt this way before," I replied, as honestly as I could. "These weeks in my new life seem to have triggered an urge. I can't say why, exactly."

"Would you mind undressing?"

"Excuse me?"

"We've reached an important point. I'd like to forestall your withholding."

"But I, I'm not withholding."

"Not to worry, Mr. uh, uh, I recognize that it's involuntary. I'm not criticizing you."

"I don't see how not, of course you are."

"You've misunderstood."

"Accusing me of withholding when, why, my Doctor-General, I was just beginning to feel so loose and open."

"Yes you were, which is why we've gotten onto a more difficult level. You're onto sensitive ground. I'm simply suggesting a step which will help you push that much farther."

"Removing my clothes?"

"Yes. It will, at first, of course feel strange, slightly uncomfortable."

"I'm afraid I'll just be nervous, and embarrassed."

"We'll not be removing our bags, my friend. You needn't fear the prying eyes of anyone."

"Will you be unclothed also, Doctor?"

"Yes. I have, in fact, already removed my clothes."

"I . . . I didn't know."

"Of course you didn't. I never mentioned it."

"Have you been unclothed all along?"

"Yes I have. I find it easier this way. By undressing we shed a host of habits and fears."

"I suppose we do." I failed to hide my lack of enthusiasm. Was I ready for revelations? Was he? How could I possibly tell him the recent history of this my new life without letting him in on my dirty little secrets? Already he had his hands full with my deviance (and whatever other puzzling information he got from Flessinger and Ponz). But if, as I dearly wished, my Doctor-General was to have a chance of straightening me out (in this my new life) he'd need me to allow him the dangerous glimpses I was so afraid of giving. I swallowed my fear and doffed my clothes right there and then, without further delay.

"Lay them wherever you'd like. Take a moment to stretch."

"May I jog a bit, in place? Get the circulation going?"

"Anything you wish. I'm only a voice, as if in a dream. Take as much time as you need." I breathed deeply and swung my limbs around, feeling the touch all upon me. Sitting down, I applauded my Doctor-General's wise choice of upholstery, realizing now why he employed fabrics which were so difficult to clean.

My mind began to register a change, a titillation and excitement that might ultimately spark spontaneous revelations.

"Would you like to exercise any more?"

"Oh no, thank you, I feel quite ready."

"Are you comfortable?"

"Yes I am, thank you."

"And are you naked?"

"Yes. I'm glad you asked me to undress."

"Why is that?"

"I just mean it feels right to be lying here naked with you."

He paused, just for a breath, then: "Tell me about your fantasies." I heard him stirring, there where he sat. Was he pale and hairless like soap? That beautiful Arabian boy came to mind, the one on film, the one whose image I had wed to my pleasure. His skin was like honey, so amber and sweet.

"I have no fantasies," I lied (thinking to myself: only films).

"What about Dexter?"

"That wasn't a fantasy. That was . . . sometimes I remember him."

"Do you masturbate?" he pried.

"Only alone, by myself." I felt him bristle at my insolence.

"Do you work with your appropriate fantasies?"

"Work?"

"You know, do you masturbate to appropriate fantasies before indulging in your inappropriate ones?" He'd given me very specific instructions about this. He scolded my silence by scooting his chair forward till I could smell the odor of his leg.

"Sometimes. Sometimes I forget." I blushed warmly with embarrassment. It wasn't my fault. The Ministry had given me the substance of my most inappropriate fantasy *and* the circumstance to act on it. If I'd been busy with something time-consuming and conducted in public maybe then I'd not have had so much time alone in which to think about the smoothness of that Arabian boy's skin, and the lovely way his cock bucked and jumped when he came all running and hot into his hand. It was alarming how many times a day I actually did put other things aside to lay down among my covers and bring him to mind.

I heard my Doctor-General scribbling a series of notes and flipping the pages of his small pad. "Are they bad?" I asked. "My fantasies?"

"Do you think they're bad?"

"I feel guilty about it."

"Is that bad?"

"Yes. It feels bad right now." What was that warmth? The Doctor-General's gaze? He cast it through the cotton of his bag, enveloping me in a reordering principle as palpable and warm as the sun's rays.

"You do know right from wrong." he surmised. "You simply need the *presence* of mind to act on it."

"I can work on it," I mumbled back to him. Really, my mind seemed altogether *too* present. And, at present my mind was on boys. The Doctor-General had no reply. Sweat from my back made the cushions bunch and cling to me. I shifted my body, uncomfortable in the prolonged silence. "What are you thinking?" I finally asked, whispering like some coquettish tart.

My doctor coughed. He slid his chair back, as if frightened by a hideous bug. I heard him steady his breathing. "What are you thinking?" he then replied.

It was a comfort knowing that beyond our sanctum sat the outer chamber, through which I would inevitably pass, and outside that the Ministry proper, its long marble hallways silent on this early Sunday morning. The city lay beyond that, wrapped in its icy frost, the children and families still in their nightclothes. Gathered around big breakfasts in warm front parlors, they looked across the glorious hills to the ocean and the bright curved horizon. However deep into my person we might delve together, however puzzling the picture of things painted by the Doctor-General and his questions, it was always there surrounding us, placing us within a wider frame, an elevation.

I sometimes wonder what it would be like to live in the woods, alone, in the hills above the city. Though I could never actually do it, there is some attraction in the idea of a warm campfire, good coffee brewing in a tin pot on it, and the perspective such a vista might offer of the city itself. Forgetting practicality for a moment, it is easy to imagine the calm and regenerative effect of a solitary interlude in the woods. One might discover, after all, something new. One might stumble across an as-yet uncataloged flower, minerals unchained from the seabed, a new color perhaps, or an ordering principle easily the rival of the Doctor-General's powerful tool. Aren't the woods organized differently than we, that is, the city? Perhaps there is something to be learned.

Just the other day, in lieu of my morning's writing, I took the tram to the Vista and walked in the woods to the north. The trees were well into their fall turning, many of them golden; whole hillsides turned a vibrant yellow, brushed with fiery strokes of red where the sap gum grew. What impressed me most was that they should have turned so resolutely and in concert, each tree sensing the change in season through no visible signal. The trees are always in fashion, never a moment out of step. The woods have no need for a clumsy vanguard modeling the new look. The fast approaching changes of the season are, among trees, signaled with far more elegance and restraint.

I believe it is possible to learn from them, to refine our own fashion system so it more nearly replicates the perfection of the trees. The clumsy means by which changes are now announced (the photo opportunities, government pageants, ministerial banners, and such) could gradually disappear (or become invisible) so that, as in the forest, change will come in concert, with no apparent coercion or leadership. Of course, the pageants, etc., will never *actually* disappear. Men are not blessed with the trees' simple, direct sensitivity to the passage of time. We get bogged down, somehow, and fail to notice a decade's passing, say, the ending of one epoch and the beginning of another. Some signal will always be needed, some colorful announcement to catch our eyes. But a certain refinement might render these signals less visible. The bluntness and noise of the orchestrated signposts could, with effort, be steadily diminished into imperceptibility. As the citizens grow used to them, I believe, as we gradually lose our ability to discern what it is that motivates us, only then will change seem to come as a spontaneous act, the city shifting in concert, just as the woods do, turning through their endless seasons.

Already it is at work. Only the Ministry really knows the mechanism by which the fashion system shifts us forward and instructs us. The average citizen enjoys the illusion of choice. Whether this is progress is a question better left to philosophers. I mean only to consider the example of the trees and to assert that their model is an advance on ours. It more nearly accomplishes what we have set out to do. The woods offer, I'm sure, countless other lessons, but this was the one that occurred to me on my recent visit north of the Vista.

Some two weeks later, my Doctor-General frowned when I told him how little I was writing. I whispered my confession over hors d'oeuvres at his favorite high-priced café, where we sat one day having lunch. I'd never seen him so effusive in his dress. He sat festooned in a white blazer, a thick linen napkin tucked into the tight neck of his bright shirt (and with pants to match). Unawares, one might easily have taken him for a pimp or quack, some unsavory lowlife in any case, allowed to sit in this swank café by dint of cash only. But he was my Doctor-General, inexplicably tacky and brash.

The day bounced brightly off him, the cold sun trebled in its severity by the intensifications of his cheap suit. We sat outside on the terrace. The wind raised devils of rubbish and dust and played havoc with my hairdo. The lunch was meant as some sort of reward or enticement, and I found myself feeling guilty. I didn't deserve his generous rewards, having engaged in nothing but deception since our last meeting.

"I just can't get myself to sit still and do it," I finally stammered. "Is there some sort of school, a writing school, I could attend?" He stared back at me, working the tine of his fork by fits and starts into the decorative metal filigree of our tabletop.

"Still waters run deep," he offered mysteriously. "You'll find the really good work, the mother lode, comes painfully slow. Classes won't help. It's like surgery, you know. Any hack can chop off a few dozen limbs on the battlefield, but the really important surgeries are tiny and painstaking, nearly invisible. Your output may be minuscule, but its impact could be far-reaching. As with surgery, life can be altered in a way that gross removal of limbs can never hope to match."

"I see."

"Severed nerves, pineal glands, and such."

The change of topic was welcome. "Don't lost limbs alter a life too?" I prompted.

"Oh, of course they do, I'd never deny that. One can, however, adjust, you see. A serviceable prosthesis, maybe just a cane. The point being, you can continue with your life, slower perhaps, impaired, but still your life. The brain surgeries, even some of the glandular surgeries can succeed in so changing you that life after is entirely new, the dysfunctional patient is made functional, perhaps for the first time. He emerges not simply as an altered version of what he once was, but as a new person." The thought cheered him. I poured our tumblers full with the amber cognac, and smiled at my generous Doctor-General.

"You can easily see the parallel in your own profession. Your guilt about page numbers must stop. What more can I say? Your efforts are exemplary. Remember that your pain is a sign of your progress." That was some small comfort. "Is it lonely?" he asked now.

"Is what lonely?" He was imagining me, perhaps, in my bedroom struggling with Appropriate Masturbation.

"Your new life, the demands of it."

"I don't consider myself lonely."

"But do you have friends? You never mention anyone."

I did have friends. But the lobster man seemed too suspicious to name. I had, after all, met him at the Burlesque, and my attendance there was strictly top secret. I had the few people I'd met in the neighborhood, the young waiters at the bistro, that fellow from whom I bought my newspaper each day. But those were minor events, of little interest to the Doctor-General. There were the pseudonymous workers at the Salon, to whom I was known only as Mr. Sludge. They could not be mentioned.

"I don't really go out much. Writing, or, uh, not writing, is so time-consuming." I sighed discontentedly.

"Have you tried meeting *other* writers?"

The thought had never occurred to me. It seemed, in fact, thoroughly repulsive. "I'm sure they're all quite busy too, what with their writing and all."

"There are readings, writers' clubs," my doctor suggested, scribbling a note and tearing it out for me to take. "The Ministry has a list, if you'll just call this number."

"Oh. Thank you."

"You must, after all, establish a network of friends if your new life is ever to become viable." Really, I seemed to have an all too viable new life, unbeknownst to my Doctor-General.

"Will everything become more and more painful as I get better?"

"For a time. It's like a volcano; pressure must build up before the explosion."

"I see. Will there be just one explosion?"

"It's really impossible to say, given the imprecision of our techniques. The knife, my friend, the knife would end all this uncertainty." He looked toward me with compassion and (was it greed?) some inspecific longing, pointing the bent tine of his fork toward my temple. The waiter hovered behind him, gently lowering the heavy tray to its resting place. He drew the resplendent metal dome away to reveal our roast.

"But the knife won't be possible, will it?" I asked again, uncertain whether I desired a yes or a no.

"No, not legally, not in our lifetime."

The sunshine bobbled and bounced around us, reflecting off the windows of the passing tram. It dappled the cobblestones and played in the wind-blown puddles left by the last week's rains. The trees on the hillsides to the east were almost bare. Small groups of old maple and alder still clung to their fiery skirts. I turned to view them directly and saw a puzzling cluster of stripes high up on the ridge. It was a banner, the same I had seen by the evening firelight several weeks previous, flying now in the bright sunshine of this glorious fall afternoon. I hesitated for just a moment and then turned away, not telling my Doctor-General of the sight. The memory of her song was too clear to have been only imagined that night. Students and old men bustled by, bumping each other in their haste. Among the last of one little bunch was the lobster man. He spotted me from several yards away but said nothing. I was glad for his uncharacteristic discretion and simply stared past him as if through air.

I would have worked, that next cold, listless morning, but I was hungry and bored, so I left, slamming the apartment door with such force that the dusty bell of my idle black typing machine rang in reply. The streets were crowded, the trams busy in both directions, and I had considerable trouble securing a table in the Café Eichelberger. Most of the men were simply in for a muffin and black coffee, a quick cigarette before reporting to work. They had their papers propped up before them, blocking any decent view of their faces. As fast as they finished they would be replaced by another, indistinguishable except, perhaps, by the variety of muffin they chose. I opened the paper and laid it out on my table, setting my hot chocolate and bread on it.

"Trespassers Sought," one headline read above a brief story at the bottom of the second page.

A small group of men is sought in connection with repeated instances of trespass in the municipal park north of the Vista. On four occasions in the last two weeks, Parks Rangers have reported the discovery of freshly extinguished fires and stanchions for the emplacement of large banners. Analyses of the stanchions have revealed no further clues to the identity of the men.

Parks Ranger scout Tom Hobbes added that numerous sightings were made of actual fires-in-progress, but that the perpetrators eluded capture on all occasions. "The group in question operates at night and seems to gather for some occult or religious purpose, or so we suspect," Hobbes said. "On each occasion we've found ritual objects and tattered cloth at the site. I've heard reports of chanting or singing, but that's still unsubstantiated." Hobbes declined to describe the objects or cloth, citing the need for secrecy in the ongoing investigation.

Anyone with information about these incidents is asked to contact the Parks Rangers Service or the Ministry of Art and Religion.

I washed the dry bread down with a warming mouthful of chocolate, mulling over this interesting bit of news. It was certainly the same group I had seen in the evening after my therapy. It seemed odd that the singing had not been confirmed, obvious as it had been to me. But perhaps that was a trick of the winds (their voices being carried clearly to the empty avenue, yet obscured in the woods much nearer to their campfire). If the Parks Rangers or the Ministry knew what song they'd been singing the nature of the case would be quite changed, I thought. Of course, it was purely an accident that I'd heard it at all. I could've been walking somewhere else, or chosen to take the empty tram and then not heard a thing. It was barely audible as it was, a whisper, a distant whistling through the trees. It might not even have been what I thought. It seemed useless to call the Ministry with information that could so easily prove to be false. I'd be in some trouble then, with the Doctor-General, leading the Ministry off on a wild-goose chase.

I washed that thought away with another mouthful of chocolate.

In the late morning, that morning, the day having turned bitter and gray whilst I sat in my kitchen peeling beets, the little bells by my door rang unexpectedly, meaning someone downstairs wanted me. It was a messenger, dressed gaily in his tight blue uniform with the little round cap and its bonbon. I invited him in and offered up a cup of tea to quell his chills.

The small package was from the Ministry. My name and address was scrawled across its top in the Doctor-General's indecipherable hand. I bade the boy loosen his buttons and relax for a bit, which he did. His pale cheeks were bright red from the cold and he smelled of sweat and exertion. A trail or two dripped suggestively down his neck and onto his chest which, I now saw as he unbuttoned his clinging shirt, was smooth and hairless. There was a note in the box from my Doctor-General.

> I'm sorry to report that progress with the technicians has been judged to be too slow. You'll be continuing with the regular course of therapy, both there and with me, but I would like to ask you to supplement that program. I've enclosed one of our home kits for you to get started with before our next session. Please read the instructions carefully and bring your first tape tomorrow.

"What is it?" the boy asked, sticking his nose into my business.

"It seems to be from my doctor," I told him. "I'm not sure yet what it is exactly." He clambered up off the couch and took the small box from me.

"There's a tape recorder in here, and some spools of tape." He pulled the items out and held them up for me to see. "And another note, or a brochure or something." This he handed over, plainly more interested in the mechanism than the note.

"Boredom Tapes," the paper was titled. "Follow instructions exactly" it warned:

> The Boredom Tapes provide a therapy designed to reinforce the enjoyment of appropriate sexual fantasies while simultaneously diminishing the appetite for inappropriate fantasies. You will be asked to masturbate to both kinds of fantasies during the course of the therapy. Accordingly, you must first find an appropriate, dependable setting in which to masturbate.

I looked over at the boy. He'd set one of the spools onto the machine and was looking for a plug. He held a flask of amber liquid in one hand, evidently procured from my package.

> When you have chosen a setting, prepare the tape machine by placing the first spool on the left and threading it, as indicated. The machine is preset to run at the correct speed and for the appropriate duration. Make yourself comfortable.

"This is wild," the boy said to me, laughing. "They sent you a bottle of massage oil." He held up the opened flask and showed me the label.

"It's good stuff, you know." He let a bit dribble over his delicate golden necklace onto his chest, where he rubbed it in with a warm hand. I could see the palpitations of his heart, pushing rhythmically against his skin where he'd rubbed the oil in. "What's with the tapes?" he asked. I read the instructions out loud to him:

> Start the tape when you are ready. Begin reciting an appropriate sexual fantasy as you masturbate yourself using an ample amount of lubricant. Enough lubricant must be used for the masturbatory activity to be audible on the tape. This is very important. The appropriate sexual fantasy you narrate should include a period of nonsexual affection leading up to foreplay and ultimately, sexual activity. The partner must be fully and repeatedly described during the course of the masturbation, and should be of an appropriate age and sex. Continue your recitation and masturbation until orgasm. At that point you may stop the tape.

My friend was clearly excited by the instructions. He chortled and blushed, playing his hands nervously across his ribs, and pressing, on occasion, at the belt of his pants. There was another page to go:

> *Immediately* upon completion of the first tape, place the second spool on the machine. Begin masturbating while reciting an inappropriate sexual fantasy. Lubricant must, again, be used in sufficient quantities

to allow monitoring of the masturbatory activity. Subject must not lapse into silence during the second tape. At all times, description must be given out loud, recounting the inappropriate sexual fantasy. Continue until the end of the tape (app. 45 min.).

I pulled his shirt back off his slight shoulders, letting my hand drift down across his nipples. His heart was beating clearly by the small hollow of his sternum. I ran my hand down past it, along the linea alba toward his belly button. His mouth was partly open. His tongue, uncertain of where to go, hung slightly over his lower teeth, wetting his full lips. He began undressing me, pulling my hand down onto his belt buckle. My thumb slipped in under the white elastic of his underpants, there where they rode slightly above his pants, and I undid his buckle and tugged, letting his big penis free from the clothes that had restrained it. His wild black hair was repeated in a softer, thick tangle above his warm erection. I looked again into his eyes, wet black pools, then put the pulsing length of his penis in my mouth. He groaned and buckled, pressing the tape machine, and pulled my last garments off me. We fell down together, his gangly warm body spread and splayed all over me, our two forms arranged in reverse, head to toe. The wet head of his penis kept pushing up across my eyebrow, catching itself on my lips and charging eagerly forward. I held it warm and strong in my mouth and pulled him closer. He played his mouth all over my belly and thighs. We explored this arrangement for some time before I finally turned to him and whispered my concern that the tape should be done properly.

Forgive me if I go back and say it did not happen. I willed that we should embrace and tangle there upon the orange carpet. I did all I've said except, finally, reaching to his shirt to pull it down off his shoulders. The well-mannered messenger boy sat, it is true, with a spot of oil on his pale chest and I did rise, walking toward him, the spools ready to be turned on, but I couldn't reach as far as his loose shirt, and instead walked past to the kitchen and put on more water for tea. He seemed about to rise, but hesitated when I slipped past him.

"Would you like some more tea?" I called, swallowing the sweet and pure desires that crowded my throat.

"Yes, but I've got to finish my deliveries." He stood by the davenport, the confused look of an abandoned dog on his face, pushing and rearranging his shorts. "They've got me on a timetable, wouldn't you know." I wondered now what had compelled me to invite him in, and why I'd chosen to read aloud the bizarre instructions sent to me by my Doctor-General. Clearly it had frightened or confused him, knowing what strange ministrations the government required of me (and which I would no doubt be commencing as he left to finish his morning rounds). It is so easy to forget the innocence of children, for whom even a brassiere is scandalous. What could he make of this lonely man and the spools of tape turning on the orders of a Doctor-General? I despised what I must seem to him to be, and felt quite at a loss to correct the misimpression.

"Needn't I sign anything, or pay?" I groped for some formal exchange by virtue of which to erase the confounding and multifarious one we'd had.

"Uh, yeah, you gotta sign my sheet," he said, buttoning his shirt back up and scanning the davenport for his work board. "Right there by number three." He pointed, his dark eyes dancing around uncertainly.

"My real name?"

"Yeah, of course, or whatever." He kept glancing at me—at the machine, looking toward the curtained windows and the small stain on the davenport where he'd let the oil drip from his hand. Had I damaged him, somehow, by my recklessness? I wanted, now, to embrace the boy, to hold him as if to soothe what I had scarred.

I felt my arms reach toward him, to wrap him up with me and show my true heart, but I flinched and drew back. It was all the same, my embraces all baffling two-edged swords that might cut him both coming and going. What possible gesture was there left?

"Is there anything I can get you, anything you need?" He was clueless, as puzzled by this solicitation as by my ardor.

"We're not supposed to take tips, if that's what you mean."

"You'll not be too cold out there? You could take my coat."

"Don't sweat it." He moved toward the door. "I'm fine, really."

"But if you change your mind." He shook his head again. "I'm home all morning, if there's any problem."

"Yeah, thanks. Maybe I'll be seeing you." Closing my apartment door gently, he disappeared into the gray day from whence he had come.

I was left in my empty room with the opened bottle of lubricant and the spools, one threaded and ready in the machine. I was hardly in the mood now to complete the awful project, overcome as I was by the desire to somehow wrest from this boy confirmation that he, and by implication then I, was okay.

On the mantel among the instructions and the morning's delivery, my ivory heirloom clock ticked steadily on. I stirred some more sugar into my tea and thought about the prospect of the spools. The mood had passed, that much was certain; I couldn't imagine lying down among my rumpled sheets to perform. The whole apartment seemed tired and dirty. Chairs were scattered all out of place, and the carpet was covered with newspapers and books. My furniture and "things" had all been turned slightly off balance, as if by an emanation (the force of my discomfort warping along the walls). I threw everything else aside and passed the day cleaning my nest to its very bone.

It was near dusk by the time I trundled the last load of boiled laundry upstairs from the basement to my now scrubbed and orderly home. I ironed the last wrinkles into oblivion, and tucked the warm, flat board back into its storage space. Everything was clean and in its proper place. The walls were bright, the carpet tamed. There was no dust, nor any old food to foul the table and shelves. I'd put the demonic taping machine in a box and labeled it neatly. I placed it by my writing desk, where it could sit without disturbing the room's delicate order. What I wanted now was to dress myself in smart, conservative clothes and go out, so that I might have the pleasure of returning to find my home clean and unblemished. Vaguely, I thought, I might then begin anew.

I tucked a muffler snugly around my neck and set out into the evening. The tower bells surprised me by ringing four times and then stopping short. It seemed dark enough to be five or six. Perhaps the municipal library would still be open. I was engaged in a rather delicate operation, or so it felt to me, nurturing a mood and resolve by walking, strolling rather, with a relaxed, if alert, gaze. To wander, take in, breathe evenly, consider the library's façade in this wintry dusk, eventually to return, though unhurried . . . Then, only then, the evening's chilly air clinging to my felt coat, the blood rosy in my fresh-scrubbed cheeks, could I turn the key in the door and cross the threshold into a new beginning. Perhaps I'd even sit easily at my desk and slip a clean white sheet into the rolling mouth of the typing machine . . .

The street was empty. A dog barked and the bark echoed against the buildings. The air was frozen, but it carried the warm smell of evening meals being cooked, garlic frying, soups simmering. A mist of pale pink light wed the city to the bay. Was it dusk? I stood looking into it for some few minutes. The ironwork of the bridges was softened by this peculiar trick of light and they looked to be standing centuries distant, silent and flat above the churning waters.

I walked on, into the noise and clamor of the market square. The vendors called out their last, lowest prices, trying to get rid of whatever they had left. Three boys filled their worn baskets with beets scarred by rot and spoilage. An old woman beside them haggled over squash. This was the time of the poor and indigent, after the day's commerce had cleaned out whatever could be sold for higher prices. The merchants were not stingy at this time of day. They set prices that brought no profit, indeed, that only minimized their loss, and they heaped the baskets full, not bothering to weigh and calculate.

There was nothing for me there and I wandered away, letting the noise and aroma diminish behind me. Where had that boy gone, guided by his schedule of deliveries? Was he still at work, cold and tired now, looking forward to a hot bath at home? Or maybe an evening of steam and massage lay ahead, at the sauna? An evening of soft towels with that slight diesel smell—fluffy and white, wrapped around his slim body. Juice was served, icy cold, by a smiling, muscular young man, and the patrons, young and old, men and women, would all smile back. Was it the messenger boy I was searching for? My route circled the apartment, where we'd met, in an ever-widening spiral.

There was a glimpse, his posture in silhouette, rushing away from the news kiosk. The figure slid down the hill toward the harbor, as if late for some rendezvous . . . What gay colors the yachtsmen strung from their double masts; the little lanterns glowed bright above the inky bay. Strings of light trailed toward me, rippling across the water. They wobbled and broke, and I felt dizzy and moved on. Near to the grand hotel a small orchestra gathered. Fur wraps and woolen scarves kept the players warm. A barrel of fire was blazing by the pit where they sat. I wanted nothing to do with the crowd. Chattering families with skating blades rushed around me, elbowing toward the ice rink. Children in stretched mufflers and riotous colors whirled too fast around the ice. I paused by a coffee vendor. His cart was the only still point within reach. He ground the beans fresh and it made a dark, warm smell more satisfying than the drink. The news vendor came by, hawking the evening edition, but he ignored my coins.

My circuit continued along its spiral. I focused my attention ahead, on distant postures, heads and hats, looking for the round cap and its bonbon. The futility of it was obvious. It became clear that if I *was* searching for the boy, I was also heading toward a familiar destination. On this journey I would not find calm and resolve (as I imagined I needed). And I would never find the lost boy, nor the gesture of reassurance I wanted to give him. It wasn't possible to find those things now, here in this city. Here I had only Lucrezia, and it was to her door that I finally come.

When I turned the corner at the Fish Street my breath quickened. There were a dozen men (two towering glamours among them) milling around the cellar door, waiting to be let in. I hesitated by the corner, feeling unreasonably "caught," then joined them.

Through the door, lanterns glowed red in alcoves dug out like dwarf apses. A blind man in leather and chiffon pressed his card into my hand, asking for money. I gave him a few coins and moved into the room. The low ceiling and thick walls kept the noise in, and I could only move forward by pivoting and turning. I got pushed up, then stood on the tattered seat of a cane chair. I could see the line of low gaslights strung across the lip of the stage. Towering hairdos shifted and waved, obscuring my view. Then the chair was pushed over and lost, crushed beneath a tide of bodies moving forward. Scuffling, whispers, then a hush and silence . . .

And there was Lucrezia! The limelight upon her, cables supporting her enormous ears, her hairdo hung from above on sky hooks. She was wrapped in yards of purple silk, miles of silk, bunched up around her prosthesis, pinned to the walls by iron spikes the railroad men brought in. Within it she danced, writhing and twisting to her own muffled song. The silk bunched and grabbed at her moving hips, twisted round her slight ankles, as she moved forward toward us. No matter that her mouth was buried behind the shimmering fabric; everyone there knew her song by heart and was singing with a lust and strength trebled by the fact of the regulations that prohibited it ... Was it mere hours, or whole ages which then passed with the night? Dawn came.

I could describe the pure exhaustion then, when the sun crawled from out of its bed and hung like a metal disc in the eastern sky, when the long chaotic night had ended and the cellar disgorged us, tumbling us out onto the empty cobblestones. I saw the gray light sink into the filthy morning mist, and our delirious breath through rasping, hoarse throats. Was it like the exhaustion of coming many times and never quite sleeping? My body had dissolved, like when your flesh is numb from sex and still you keep at it until the numbness is a tingling and, finally, a sensation. Numbness is sensation. The costume hides you and it exposes you to the world. It imprisons you and it sets you free.

I could tell you that we never stopped singing. The magic of Lucrezia twisting in the limelight, those rolling waves of music, beauty ... there I found my communion, my ecstasy.

I could take you with me, walking with the lobster man, returning to our apartments, drenched and drained from the evening. "I dress as her sometimes," he tells me. "At home."

Imagine him. The lobster man pulls the thick curtains shut, turning the bright sunlight dark and orange. The cat cowers on the bed, watching, swiveling its tiny head back and forth. The lobster man stands naked before his secret chest of clothes. Lavender perfume is sprinkled on him like a benediction. The unholy bangs and swallowed screams of violence in the apartment above thud dully through the carpeted floor (the pulling of the organ stops, the church choir's song). The robes, the vestments. The candles are lit and the altar turned to reveal a full-length mirror of astonishing clarity . . .

"In silk. Not the quality and size of the actual costume, mind you."

"Certainly not."

"Just enough to create the illusion of a costume."

"And you sing?"

"No, no. Not then, not there," he rasped. "I imagine the song. I mouth it sometimes, but I don't take any chances."

We walked together, just as the rugby boys walk in their afternoon exhaustion and camaraderie. I see them down my street coming in from the fields. They're golden in the warmth of the day's last sunlight. Clouds of breath dance about them and the steam rises from off their muscled bodies. Their legs, under the weight of bulky torsos, have a simple finality, a gait of resignation and peace, a giving up, as of that on the face of the Christ nailed finally to his place. I could tell you the sun burned through the awful mist and shone golden against our faces.

I could describe, in short, the beauty of that night, as I could for any night with Lucrezia; there was beauty every time I saw her. It was something beyond this, though, that made that night special, something beyond Lucrezia: a meeting that I had been heading toward, a collision—a fate that overtook me in a solitary moment by the entrance door.

A slim figure blocked the door as I slipped out for some air, a hooded figure. I let him pass ahead of me, then followed out onto the dimly lit street. The door shut loudly behind us. I closed my eyes to rest them and slumped back against the stone wall. Then, a warm hand took mine and he pulled me away toward the alley.

"Come with me, Mr. Sludge," he whispered. Was it the messenger boy? And how did he know my name (that is, the name that was not my name)? I had pulled back instinctively, but gave in and followed when I heard this young voice, reedy and cracking with each nervous syllable. The hood kept his face from me. He pushed us into the alleyway.

His two hands were long and trembling, pressed against my chest to keep me by the wall. The bubbling jet of a gaslight silhouetted him, outlining his hood. He paused, then moved a step closer so I could feel his breath when he spoke. "I need your help," he brought out. "We need your help very badly."

"Yes, but what do you mean?" I touched his hands, which felt hot as fire. "And who are you?" He took me by the shoulders and turned us around. The gas flame that had silhouetted him now cast enough light for me to see his face clearly. He pulled the hood back and dropped his hands.

"Maybe you remember me?" It was the boy from the films, the slim foreign boy from the films of Flessinger and Ponz. His eyes were bloodshot and deep. Dull bruises marked his forehead and cheeks; his full lips were wet and trembling.

"I, yes. Yes, I do remember you." I tried to steady my voice. "Are you all right?" He pulled his hood up, hiding his face in the shadows.

"I'm okay," he answered, "but I don't have much time." His divinity was alive in his voice, a lilting, strangely inflected voice of unlocatable pitch and tone. Every word brushed across me, effervescent and painful. He put his hand to my neck and touched my pulse, there by my cold throat. "You've got to help us," he enjoined.

"How?" I asked, wondering, also, "Who?" He bent over, coughing, and then the gaslight went out, snuffed by someone whose footsteps echoed and then stopped.

"I must go, Mr. Sludge. Tell no one you saw me," he whispered. He held my head in his hands, pushing his warm mouth close to my ear. "Meet me, please, in the passage by the university, in one week, at eight."

"In daylight?" I asked, unwilling to let him go.

"At night," he instructed and broke free, running back down the Fish Street. I listened to him disappear into silence, then the racing of my heart took his place. No one else was around; the mysterious extinguisher of the light had stopped or had turned and fled. I stood alone, haunted by this boy, or the memory of him, so vivid and near. Already the details of his appearance were drifting away. Had he worn an overcoat? His face was marked with bruises. Or had that been a trick of the light? He was nearly as tall as me, though his wrists were slim and trembling. I remembered him naked, supine, his body flexing with the muscular waves of pleasure that came, then, bursting into his hand.

The boy was out there, and I knew that he would return. First to haunt me in my sleep, and soon, again, as flesh and blood. Only time kept him from me now.

I TOLD MY FATHER I'D LIKE TO PUT OUT TO SEA ON A FREIGHTER, THE summer when I was fifteen, to spend six years on the earth's open oceans and not pass them locked up in the secondary schools and the university.

I had read books about sailors and heard the ship's steam whistles blowing in the harbor. I would sit by the shore and watch them grow more and more distant, their horn blasts diminished down to ghostly whispers, barely audible among the calling of seabirds. What a foolish boy I was, intoxicated by the cheap romanticism of the sailor's life. The seductive lure of peril and isolation, the promise of discovery, exotic ports, and friendship. There was a drawing in my *Golden Treasury of the World's Oceans* which showed two young sailors sharing the watch on a black Indonesian night. They were perched high above the ship's deck, reclining in a small nest, pressed together, gazing out into the crystal night. The curve of the earth's edge was visible where it met the night sky. It was all I ever wanted. The nearness and warmth of a friend sharing that privileged view.

There were several months during which I made plans, regarding this fantasy as a real alternative. I plotted out a means to realize it, with or without my family's blessing. It was the year after

Herman had left, and I was very soured on the old district. The energy and time I'd spent on that obsession was free to be turned to my new plan of escape. I acquired pamphlets by mail from shipping companies whose names I'd seen at the loading docks. Pamphlets about anything: shipping prices, storage techniques, yearly stock reports (so I'd be familiar with the whole operation). In the afternoons I watched the boats, sitting on a bench by the municipal pier, or sometimes from a clearing up on the bluffs. I never spoke with a sailor or a captain, or with anyone for that matter. My plans were top secret, and were only finally revealed when I took my father into my confidence.

I gathered my courage and said one night that I was going to sea and what did he think. We were sitting together in the front parlor, a bright fire dancing and spitting on the irons. My stomach was all butterflies and nervous, wondering what he'd say now that I'd let my secret out.

"What was that?" he asked, looking up from his lecture notes.

"I'm leaving school, to go to sea," I said quite boldly. I hadn't the slightest idea what I wanted from him, except, perhaps, simply his attention. He stared at the black windows, our reflections wrapped and warped along the old, sagging glass. I waited, patient as a teakettle boiling.

"It's quite costly, I understand. Even the fares for children."

"But I'm not going as a passenger, Daddy, I'm going as a sailor."

He looked up at me. "What an idea ... to sea as a sailor. I read a book about that once, a boy about your age running off to the piers at Southampton, finding himself work on a steamship." He drifted away into his reverie.

"But I'd like really to do it, Daddy, now." He cocked his head to one side and began drumming on the tabletop. I fidgeted in my seat and wondered how to proceed.

"Such a good story it would make, a boy like you going off to sea in a modern ship. There's such a lot of characters on these ships, I imagine, each with a host of stories to tell. What a fine idea for a book."

"I'm sure I could keep a diary."

He nodded. "Or perhaps as a memoir."

"But I've not gone yet."

"Of course you haven't, you're only still just a boy, after all."

"But I want to go, soon."

"You wouldn't mind if I try this out on some friends, would you?"

"Try what out?"

"Your little story idea, see what they think."

"Couldn't you just tell me what *you* think, tell me if you'll help me?"

"What sort of help could I give you?"

"Well." I really didn't know . . . but I *did* know this slim thread of his attention was something to cling to. "Well, just, first, talk to me about it because I don't know what I'm doing really, yet, and then help me to figure out exactly *what* to do."

"Yes, yes, of course. I think more reading would be a good idea, as preparation."

"I've done a lot of reading already," I pointed out. "Books and pamphlets and technical manuals."

"All of that?" He seemed impressed.

"But when should I actually go to sea, Daddy, when do you think I can leave school and do it?"

"You don't really want to leave school, do you?"

"Well, I . . . " The simplicity of his question made it doubly hard to answer. I knew that in fact I didn't really want to go, but also that I did not want simply to stay. I wanted to be prevented from going. I wanted to be forced back to school, made to attend against my adventurous will. "I don't want to leave school, no."

"There's so much to be learned in school," he added, touching me with his strange hand.

"But, Daddy, I don't just want to stay either." The difficult fact came lumbering out, a bitter metal chain that I hoped would—by virtue of its nakedness and truth—link me securely to his attention. Already I could sense him drifting away. "I want to run away," I added urgently, "even though I also want to be in school."

"That makes no sense," he informed me, rising from his chair. "Either you want to be in school or you don't. And I'm happy to hear it's the former." I lay down across both our chairs, filling the empty space he'd just left. I was dizzy and a bit short of breath. My father continued: "Could you maybe find an assignment that allows you to pursue this nautical interest within the boundaries set by school?"

(Intimacy was such a terribly difficult thing for me then. I groped and grabbed for it in my clumsy adolescent way, completely stupid about other people's minds and perceptions. Just when I felt certainly on the verge of a kiss, an embrace, or some warm word and tears, my moment would turn upside down, dumping cold showers of indifference upon me. I was forever repeating, in some new variation, the terrible experience I'd had on the verge of puberty when I was invited to my first sleep over. In the absolute darkness of the basement room where we'd all camped out in sleeping bags, I had complied with the announced plan that we undress and work our little bodies up to an erotic pitch so the lights could be turned on and all of us could see each other, thus sealing our bond forever. I'd cast off everything, including my socks, and was playing my hands over my body to a pitch of delight when, at the call of the unbearably stimulating countdown from ten, we arrived at "the moment" and the lights came brightly on, revealing a room full of pajamaed boys and me, alone, naked and erect among them. I withered and shrank, jumping back into my bag to hide, and never forgave them the betrayal.)

It was like that with my father in the moment I've just described. By slow and secret signals I'd been beckoned to let him look inside me, to reveal myself as an offering to seal our bond. The confessional urge has always held, for me, that seduction. If (I kept believing) I revealed myself, some divine link would thereby be forged.

Locating the object of revelation has proven more and more impossible as I've grown older. My body no longer contains me. To be naked is not enough, is, in fact, counterproductive. I am unreadable without my costume. Sometimes I long for that impossibly distant condition, the one which my cruel peers exploited, where the unbuttoning of a shirt, the tugging down of an elastic waistband, could mean so terribly much. Now it means nothing. We routinely strip for doctors without any of the intimacy and terror we knew as children. It is a greater horror to be caught wearing the wrong outfit than to be seen naked.

I followed my father's insensitive advice and found ways to incorporate school and my fascination with sailors. Primarily I found that I might gain some satisfaction by attending school in a sailor's suit and hat. By this conceit I felt enclosed within my longing and at the same time was denied its consummation. I was a sailor forced to attend school. This fact was announced at every moment simply by virtue of my costume. I had no need to say a thing about it.

Winter came, announcing itself in a low, faceless front of bitter clouds. The flat iron sky stayed cold and flat, colored by the factory's ash. There was no wind. Breath froze and hung before our faces, waiting for us to walk through or turn away. I sat alone in my room, wondering the days away with thoughts of "the boy." Where was he? Into what dangerous life had he disappeared?

I had neglected my tapes, although they were due to be reviewed by the Doctor-General and his staff. Following my first attempt, I was given hearty congratulations and instructions to complete one each day, each week's seven to be turned in on Friday. This week I had neglected them all. My plan was to finish five this morning before my one o'clock meeting.

The tapes were a simple, if time-consuming, task. I set the spools turning on my side table, with me buck naked on a little coverlet I kept folded by my bed. You can well imagine my frustration, as early as tape two, and will understand my decision to fake it with the remaining tapes. Really, I had no choice (and no desire to let my Doctor-General know). I simply smiled and handed him the tapes, snugly buckled into their canvas satchel.

"Very good, my friend, we're all quite pleased with your work on this one." The Doctor-General took the load from my hands. "Homework is rarely done so conscientiously." I smiled my thanks and stared out the window at the terrible day.

"Will we be going into the inner chamber today?" I asked. "Or will we just stay out here and talk?" His calming gaze passed over me, taking my attention with it to each corner of the room and then, again, to the windows.

"We'll be going inside," he replied without apology.

I grunted and fiddled briefly with his specimens. A variety of rodents and some larger mammals occupied the tabletop. Their limbs were drawn out and pinned to the wooden surface. Some seemed only to be sleeping. Their little fur bodies rose and fell with each breath. Others were clearly dead. All of them sported one mark or another (evidence of the Doctor-General's interest in them)—fluid-filled tubes, vast shaven expanses, recently sewn surgical scars. It held my attention, and seemed inviting (perhaps as a subject for a painter of still lifes). The light from my Doctor-General's desk lamp raked across them, casting provocative shadows on my own skin.

"Progress is slow," he complained. "I can never get enough animals. If I'm lucky they'll grant me access to the municipal cadavers."

"What a blessing that would be." I knew nothing about the real demands of science.

"It's hell collecting these things; you'd never dream what I go through." I always imagined he had assistants who saw to such things, being practically a minister and all.

"Couldn't one of your staff do it for you?"

"And have them ask what I'm up to in my spare time? Certainly not, never in a million years. People are so close-minded about this sort of thing. Why I've had to come up with a ruse just to get the cadavers. *If* I get them."

"How unpleasant."

"You bet your life it is, masquerading as a dentist just to get my hands on some decent, fresh heads."

"I understand."

"I certainly hope you do. Really, I shouldn't have said a word. These things can wear on a man." The Doctor-General glanced at his watch and stood. "Oh well, mum's the word, as they say. Nothing leaves our little chamber, now does it?"

"No."

"Doctor/patient, and all that."

I stood, following his example, swallowed a heavy sigh, and shuffled along toward the now-open portal.

The Doctor-General was already inside, waiting, his belt buckle loosened and bag in hand. Not a word was said. The panel slid shut and the door was closed. I put my bag on and began undressing. The couch on which I lay felt already warmed, as if by another body. Its soft form was crushed and contoured to a shape unlike what I made.

"Has someone been lying on my couch?" I asked, suspicious and hurt merely by the thought of it.

"Why do you ask?"

"It feels recently warmed. And the cushions are all crushed in a strange way." I sat up again. The couch gave off a suspicious odor. "You've got your bag on, don't you?"

"Yes I do. Are you wearing yours?" His pencil could be heard tacking even as he spoke.

"Yes, of course I am. And no clothes, which is why this couch is starting to bother me. Have you been lying on it?"

"Yes I have. Sometimes I'll lie in here to rest, if I'm feeling tired." This was not as bad as I'd feared. I thought perhaps another patient was allowed to lie here, and not long before my arrival. That the Doctor-General might occasionally nap upon my spot, catching a few restorative winks, was not so terrible. I rather liked the idea of his overlarge body, weighed down by fatigue, splayed across our common dwelling place.

"Do you undress first?"

"Yes I do. I sleep for a half-hour or so before our session."

"Well, that's not so bad." I stretched back out on my stomach and let my arms drift to the floor. "I thought maybe you let someone else lie here."

"Would that bother you?" He kept scribbling.

"Oh yes, a great deal."

"Why would that bother you?" My bag had been washed. Its lemony soap smell played freshly in my nose. I thought about the creepy feeling on my skin moments before.

"They'd get the couch all dirty, and then I'd have to lie on it, probably in their sweat or something."

"Yes?"

"Who knows what they might've said, or thought, or maybe, you know, passed gas or something."

"But *I* might have soiled the couch," he interjected. "Would that also bother you?" I couldn't imagine my Doctor-General's immaculate sleep fouled by odors or indigestion. His sweat would be pure.

"I don't imagine it would smell. You're much cleaner than most people. Probably it would just evaporate into air, not soiling the sheet at all."

"Do you think you might soil the couch?" What a startling thought. My Doctor-General had such an instinct for the deft turning of a question back upon itself.

"No. I rather like my odor." His pencil scratched rapidly across the page. I pushed my nose in deep among the bunched-up cotton, sniffing, unencumbered by my earlier anxiety. It did smell, mostly like me, or rather, like my bedclothes back home. A hint of my Doctor-General's pomade was evident, enough to make me consider switching brands, its odor was so appealing. We used the same brand at the Salon. My little nipples dug against the sheet and my stomach started a sweetness that was magnified with each small thrust of my hips forward. Sometimes I wore a bag at home in bed and pretended I was here, on my Doctor-General's couch. I rolled onto my side and curled up, awaiting an inquisitive prod.

"What are you thinking now?" he asked after a prolonged silence. Then, what I least expected—an honest answer—came from my lips.

"I'm thinking about her," I volunteered tenderly.

"Her?"

"Lucrezia."

"That drag queen?"

"Yes." It was as though I'd leaped from an impossibly high balloon and was floating, now, freely through air.

"What are you thinking about her?"

"Her dress when she sang, the silk that wrapped around her."

"Yes?"

"She sings for me, it seems, each time. As though every word is meant for me and every ounce of her life is spent simply to give me her songs. She's like an animal in a zoo, or a divine god. Human beings aren't capable of what she does." I paused in my revel, wondering still what hidden pressure had pushed this, now, forward.

"What is it that she does?"

What is it that she does? I couldn't find the words. It was something very much like love, a completion of the soul, as though a large part had been missing. The world without her was plain and flat. Yet it was equally an expansion, as though a canvas bag were ripped from off my body and I was allowed to burst free. And it was a provocation. If the rebels shared any quality with her, it was this last.

"She sings each night," I finally explained. "I often go to listen."

"What does she sing?" Surely my Doctor-General was more sophisticated than that.

"She still sings many of the songs from the old theater, the ones she sang at the opera house."

"Oh, yes."

"Do you remember them, how glorious they were?"

"I do remember, yes." I, inside my bag, was misty-eyed, and wondered if my Doctor-General might be the same. She was a subject about which he'd spoken with some sophistication during our occasional meetings outside his chambers. The unsteadiness of his voice betrayed a complex emotion.

"She *was* unsettling. I believe that's why they stopped her."
The pronoun betrayed him.

"They were wrong to do it." I expected him to ask that I now
leave. Surely we'd strayed into nontherapeutic territory. I knew
now he shared my sympathies, yet could not bring himself to say
so. All he gave was his silence. I didn't interrupt it.

"Why are you telling me this?"

"You asked me what I was thinking."

"Yes I did."

"And I told you."

"Are you aware of the risk you're taking?"

"I don't think so, no."

"Let's step outside, shall we?"

I was made to register with the Parks Rangers, leaving addi-
tional information in the file that had been started for me. It was
quite simple really, a formality which acted as a warning, but it
meant the rest of my afternoon was spent shuttling between
offices, carrying with me a sheaf of papers and chemical tags. I
hadn't expected that anything real would come of my confession.
The Doctor-General was profoundly upset, more so than he perhaps realized, and he'd settled on this measure, I believe, as the
easiest way of fulfilling his ministerial duties without actually
imperiling my future.

I walked home through the blustering snow while the sun
crept down out of the sky. A few brief moments of pink and
mauve, then darkness. I walked along the shore listening to the
waves slap against the stones of the seawall.

I slept heavily that night, and well into the next morning. I
rose only to make some tea (it must have been late afternoon)
before returning to bed and a disturbing collision of dreams and
half-waken perceptions. I felt feverish and soporific. Snow
obscured the windows. Days passed, it seemed, and I couldn't

rouse myself from bed. Was it a virus or sickness? Finally, one morning, I woke to bright sunshine glaring through the frosty windows. It turned my room a brilliant white and startled me.

I'd slept through the weekend. Outside, children ran down the icy lane in their heavy boots and slid recklessly toward the market. I was expected at the Salon by ten o'clock. Doctor Cotton had probably arrived early and might now be shoveling the drifts clear of the door.

The chairs were ready, empty and clean. My somber colleagues sat idly by, waiting for their next clients. Many of them were gathered by the big pan, gossiping about sports or noses. I slipped into my gown, pulling the hair net on, and tossed my shoes into the gray metal locker.

The buzzer rang twice, meaning a client had come in, and the three bells following told me it was mine. The beating of snow from off a greatcoat could be heard, and an exchange of pleasantries. I straightened my gown and went to the front hall, happy to begin at once. Waiting made me nervous. When I was idle, it seemed that just anyone might walk in, perhaps even my Doctor-General.

"Good afternoon, Doctor," my client said warmly. He always called me "doctor." "Afternoon, Minister." I bowed slightly and shook his hand. "You're looking well." The aside was important. Any man who came to our Salon had worries about his appearance. Despite confidence and self-assurance, he inevitably wanted some confirmation of his image. I would give it, reflecting back to him what he wished to be.

"You've walked?" I asked, noting the rosy glow on the minister's "cheeks" (which is to say the "cheeks" I had been constructing for him). Perhaps he had, perhaps not. Regardless, I knew this to be part of his profile. He was the minister who walked, who walked to work, who walked everywhere. He had a golden retriever, and was normally pictured with it, holding a hefty walking stick. An insensitive man would think my question stupid and not bother asking. But I knew better.

"Yes, of course, Doctor. The air is perfect today, so clean and vigorous. I'd like to think the whole city shall be walking today. The snow seems to have slowed the trams."

"A blessing."

"A blessing indeed."

We strolled together back to the big room and my chair (which I had polished hastily when the chimes rang). He settled himself, savoring one of the little hard candies I kept in a bowl beside the tool tray. There were two other clients. The bells went off again, and the adjutant wheeled a groggy man past us (having just finished him off in the Chamber of Totality). My colleagues gathered around the client, a short, recently bearded man, barely conscious.

"Always busy," the minister observed, "though you seem never to lose your calm."

"Thank you, sir. You're a keen observer." I strapped him into the chair and checked around me for mirrors. Someone had stupidly left one open, and quite near his face. I snapped it shut before he could sneak a glance. It was my fault for not checking. God forbid that a client should see his unconstructed face in the middle of the work, with all the struts and fills removed. It can undermine the whole illusion if the bearer does not believe the face to be more or less "real." (Who knows what subcutaneous musculature might sag or fold in dismay with the brief remembrance of the actual face. Whole ornaments might shift out of position, apple cheeks turn to sauce, dimpled chins become unbordered craters if that troubling thought is let loose to trigger the small, muscular twitch—often the only outward sign of such hidden doubts—that will then undo what we've so carefully done.)

"How are those jaws today, sir?" I poked gently at my last week's work, a jawline that was roughly a composite of our last three Wilderness Ministers, two lumberjacks, and a Siberian husky. My client hoped to become the next Wilderness Minister, and was due to have his face in the papers nearly every day. Rumor had it that several winter pageants would feature him, following the progress of his jaw and hairline, both of which I would be overseeing.

"Strong, Doctor, strong. Just this morning I cracked a walnut with them."

"Very impressive, sir."

"Photo op, you know. I didn't want to be seen just standing around." I cut through the false putty "jaw" and pulled the little capsules out. They had expanded quite as far as they could without bursting through the surface. Each week I added new and larger capsules that would expand slowly over seven days and then, when about to break, be replaced by the next set. His picture needed to appear frequently throughout this "enlargement" so that no one would be shocked by the metamorphosis. Eventually a permanent structure would be welded on, but that had to wait.

I pulled the loose putty off his face. Emptied of the capsules it formed an unattractive ditch running from his ear to his chin. He reached instinctively toward it. Happily, I'd drawn the restraints tight. I smiled confidently at what was left of him, a pale, withered envelope of flesh not recently exposed to the sun. He coughed and squinched around in his chair, obviously a bit disturbed by the work. "Been getting some sun, Minister?" I asked to draw his attention away. He blushed, curling his thin lips into a smile.

"I've been doing quite a bit of walking . . . in our lovely wilderness." He was delighted by the thought. "You know, I've always loved the woods, ever since I was a boy . . . I'd go walking with my dog."

"A fine, strong dog."

"Yes, yes, a heroic dog. Noble, smart. He saved me once, or I saved him."

The minister drifted off like the snows, a misty bliss in his dull blue eyes, his mind now at play in the fields of his most wished-for memories. I moved quickly to do my part, constructing for him the face that would make it so. The capsules and putty were quite simple. I slapped them together on the counter and returned, slipping in from behind to caress his jaw. I pressed the crude construction into place.

Something about the rest of him troubled me. We had ignored the nose and brow (at the client's request), but I knew in my heart that this was not wise. If the face were to work completely, it mustn't be divided.

"Sir?"

"Yes, Doctor . . . forgive me if I was snoozing."

"I prefer it. You're a busy man. I'm happy if you can find time to rest."

"It's so tiring, all of this . . . walking."

"Yes, I'm sure it is. I wondered if we might discuss your face for a moment."

"Certainly, Doctor, by all means. There's nothing *wrong*, is there?"

"No. Nothing we can't fix. Your jaw is growing beautifully. I'm just concerned that we're not doing enough."

"Speak to me, tell me."

"I believe in your goal, but we can't go on ignoring your nose. It can only get worse as the rest of your face grows."

"But this was my mother's nose, Doctor. It's all I have left of her."

"I see. Could we perhaps have a mold of it made and preserved? You could wear it at home, or whenever you're out of the public eye."

"And what about the nose on my face?"

"At the very least, simple enlargement to avoid the appearance that your nose is shrinking."

"Yes, and ideally?"

"Ideally, we could match the composite jaw to a nose derived from the same sources, and then grace it with the appropriate brow."

"I don't know, Doctor. I might need to ask the Prime Minister's counsel." I brushed some dust out of his nasolabial fold. I was glad he thought the question serious enough to warrant such attention.

"The work should begin this week."

"Not much time then."

"No, I'm afraid not. A little paint and powder should see you through until Friday, but after that, I can't promise anything."

I finished his face, sealing the jaw off and brushing up the shadowed folds. His hairline was doing well. We'd begun with a simple change in style, combing his hair back to expose the high forehead and create the impression of tremendous acceleration forward. He always seemed to be going somewhere. A quick steam and a spray, then I flipped the glorious mirrors open at last. I patted him proudly on the shoulder and bade him good day.

The shadow—that boy—hovering in the margins this long week now slipped free and enveloped me, expanding to fill every corner of our city and the night. He was lurking, hiding behind the rubbish, scuttling through the alleyway, moving slowly toward our promised rendezvous. Could he be living in the city? His nervousness and fright, his quick disappearance, said he was a fugitive. I imagined finding him, this time hurt, barely conscious, and bringing him back with me to minister to his wounds. It would be awful, but it was what I wanted more than anything.

I put on my black felt coat and buttoned it up, turning the collar against my skin. There were some cigarettes by the lockers and I stuffed them in my breast pocket, thinking he might want one. I really had no idea who he was, or how it had come to this.

I walked uphill toward the university, listening to my boots in the snow. There was little else, just my breathing and heartbeat when I'd stop to rest, the water moving far below in the channel, perhaps some wind somewhere, maybe in the hills.

All the children were safe at home now, damp and exhausted from their daytime play. They were dry and pajamaed, lying about on parlor rugs by fires, playing card games and reading. Mothers bent near to hot chocolates, readying the tiny marshmallows that, no matter how stale, would delight their sleepy tongues. If I could lie unnoticed among them, small and sweet-smelling, keeping quiet and to myself, to be given chocolate and read to, finally, to be tucked in with my brothers, the eiderdown heaped high upon us, our limbs all atangle, whispering to one another in sleep, simply our breath, unheard, crossing our lips, and the warmth of the soft cheek which lay so near, sharing one pillow . . .

The bells began to ring, distant and near. It was eight, precisely. I listened, then ran, hoping the boy would not have been and gone at the stroke of the hour.

I slid along at a reckless pace, caught in the glare of floodlights mounted on the university's fortification. In the snow fresh footsteps crowded the narrow entrance to the passageway. My heart was in my throat, cold and raw from running so hard, and I swallowed, trying to catch my breath. I gazed at the lightless tunnel, then stepped forward into it. Under my boots, the hardness and grit felt strange. As I walked, my hand brushed the wall, still damp with condensation. Where was he? If I got through to the other end, I would know he wasn't here. And then what?

The light was emerging dimly ahead, where the walkway passed into the market. My heart sank to see it empty. I moved faster, wanting to get, now, to the end and confirm the awful absence. Almost running, I stumbled, tripped on a loose piece of rock, and fell sideways. Someone grabbed me from behind, wrapping his arms around my waist, and saved me from falling against the stones.

"Be careful," he admonished. It was that voice, that divine, inflected, breaking voice I'd been hearing each night before sleep. "You might hit your head." I felt I might go limp and let him carry me away, undress and bathe me, minister to my wounds, and put me to bed. But I had no wounds. His swift and beautiful arms had saved me.

"I didn't see you," I told him. "Where were you?"

"I followed you in," he answered, brushing filth from me where I'd stumbled. "I couldn't see a thing in here." It was I, this time, who trembled, familiarity having given him confidence and robbed me of it. "Do you have a match?"

The small box was in my front pocket. "Here." I pressed them into his warm palm and let our touch linger briefly. He struck the flame at once, blinding us both for a moment with its flare. "Were you followed?" he asked.

"What?"

"Did anybody follow you here?" I hadn't even thought to look.

"No, I, I don't think so." My eyes had adjusted. His face was warm and rosy in the dim light, no trace of the bruises I had seen, or thought I'd seen, a week before. Around his neck a tattered cloth bandanna hung, orange, black, and green where grease or snow had not yet obscured its colors.

"You've got to be careful now. They may know we've made contact."

"Who? Why would I be followed?" The whole truth had not yet dawned on me. "Why have you contacted me?" He lit a second match and touched its fire to a length of pitch wood. We crouched near the warm flame and its reflection danced in the black pools of his eyes. Now *he* trembled, wetting his lips to speak.

"You must help us," he implored, reaching his hand out to touch me. "We can't last another winter."

"But who are you, who are you with?"

"The opposition, Mr. Sludge, I'm with the rebels." He held the bandanna up for me to see, lifting it from his neck and placing it in my hands. It was damp with his sweat, dirty from endless weeks against his skin, tucked under a shirt for safety . . . worn proudly only in the hills among his comrades. I pressed it to my face and smelled his sour-sweet smell, like oranges (distant cousin to the powerful fumes of Flessinger and Ponz). It was a stirring record of his labors and dedication, an irrefutable argument that swayed me as no string of numbing rhetoric ever could. I pulled the cold night air through it again, into my lungs, and considered him, this slim boy with whom I now shared the warmth of a fire.

"What have I to do with the rebels?"

"You can help us, Mr. Sludge, at the Salon."

"I don't understand." It was all too much. "I don't understand how you found me." The small fire brightened as the pitch opened up and burned from inside.

"We can't stay here. Take me home with you, give me tonight and I will make it all very clear." Of course I would . . . keep him tonight from the cold and, god only knows, the Parks Rangers or worse.

"What . . . now?"

"If you will do it, give me the chance." I rose, reached out an arm, and helped him up.

How can I place myself anywhere in that moment, so wide and far did I range, carried magically on the empty flutter of my heart. My breath broke free in clouds, billowing from my open mouth, and tumbled me upward with its unfolding. One bright star hung heavy above us in the black expanse, casting a glow like the moon on a river's bank. I felt myself reclining. Clock towers turned their metal gears, bells unhinged by the lateness of the hour. They gave nothing but silence, as if the night had become so deep and dark in its turning that time itself had folded under.

We arrived home covered in a dusting of snow and crept up the empty stairs to my door. Nothing stirred, no dogs or infants wailed, no stair steps creaked at our passing. The door turned silently on its hinges and let us into the warm room.

"May I undress?" the boy asked, "and leave my things to dry?"

"Yes," I whispered, reaching to unbutton his overcoat. "I'll get us some blankets."

The films had not been made too long ago. His body, made soft and darker by the dim light, still held that animal grace and power evident in his manipulations on screen. The line of his thighs was as long and smooth as it had there seemed, graced with an almost invisible blessing of silken hair. He was still proportioned as a puppy is, lanky and slim, his muscles still soft and rounded. I was confused and speechless. I undressed too, hanging my clothes with his to dry by the heater, and wrapped myself in a blanket. He stood naked in the warm dark room, seemingly unaware of (or, perhaps, simply undisturbed by) the effect he had upon me.

"What have you got to eat around here?" he asked. The low

bedside light cast shadows on his belly. He was a brash and confi-
dent boy, cocky and self-assured despite his vagrant life. I nodded
uncertainly and looked toward the kitchen. He moved about the
apartment competently, finding spoons and a pan, fishing things
from my icebox without any further direction from me. I watched
the small muscles of his ribs, the tenderness of his slim frame,
and held him all over in my eyes. What dangers threatened him,
what sharp weapons might ultimately tear this young skin? My
heart and hands ached to move over him. Would I be asked to
join the rebels? I watched him walk toward me with food and tea
for us both. A delicate ripple of muscle ran across the soft plane
of skin inside from his hips, there atop his long thighs. He sat
beside me, crossing his naked legs, and leaned close to tell me the
story of how he came to be in this room, now, with me.

"You don't need to know about my family. There's nothing to
know. I wasn't born in this city, or lived here, before I came a few
years ago, and then I came on my own. I had quit school and, you
see, I don't really remember my life before."

"Why don't you remember?"

"There's nothing. I was small; I grew up. I came here on a
train, with a man I gave favors to. I had nothing really, except this
man, and I left him when the train came here. It was warmer
then, springtime."

"Last spring?" He nodded. "I wasn't here then. I came back at
the end of summer."

"I know that."

"How? How did you know I was—that I am 'Mr. Sludge'?"

"We know. We know the Salon. The rebels had you placed
there."

"The lobster man."

"And we made the films."

"The rebels made the films?"

"We are involved."

"Flessinger and Ponz?"

"I don't know the names. The man who shot the films was with us. That was my first contact. He was the policeman who had me arrested last summer when I was vagrant."

"After you left the man on the train?"

"I slept in boxes by the harbor. The policeman gave me a choice."

"He made you perform in the films?"

"It was a choice he gave me. Either that or jail, or school I think."

"Tell me about the films."

He had finished the soup I gave him and now lay beside me curled in blankets. The small rise of his bare ankle, there where his foot stuck out from the blankets, kept my attention.

"There was a platform, a piece of plywood I think, on bricks to raise it off the ground and I was put there with a rug. I had no instructions except a clock, you see, and fifteen minutes' time, so long as I could be seen by the camera. It wasn't difficult."

"I didn't know there was a platform."

"Can't you see it on the film?"

"No." I smiled at his alarm. "It's all close-up. You're just sitting, or lying there, in your place."

"I wanted them to show the platform. What else is shown?"

His question was vain, but his vanity intrigued me. "They start with your back, and then, you know, all of you, and you face the camera. It's out of focus."

"All of it?"

"Just the very start, until you turn, and then it's all clear, all very detailed."

"And . . . it gets to you?"

"Oh yes, absolutely." I blushed thinking of it.

"I've wanted to see it, but I can't, now that he got me out of there."

"Who got you out of there?"

"He has no name. I can't say his position, but he got me out a few months ago."

"What does that mean?"

"He gave me my new task. I did not want it at first, but it was made inviting. He was very slick. He had me figured inside and out. That's how they do it, you see, that's how the rebels do it. They know what you want more than anything else and then they give it to you."

"What did he give you?"

"Well, what do you think?" The boy simply stared.

"I have no idea. An adventure? Some independence?"

"Yes."

"More?"

He shrugged and left only silence to answer my question. "You know I need your help," he finally said.

"How?"

"You'll be working on the Prime Minister soon."

It was outlandish. "I don't believe you."

"Believe me. He will ask for you at the Salon."

"He's obviously not going to ask for *me*."

"No, no. He *will* ask for you. The Prime Minister must have a man who is not savvy about politics, someone with no concern for those things. That's why we placed you there."

"I don't see why he'd want such a man."

"Because he has something to hide. He needs you because he knows you're competent, and because you wouldn't care if he was . . . a general or, or a traitor. Something is secret for him and we don't know what it is."

"And I'm to find this out?"

"That's my plan."

"*Your* plan?"

"I keep my eyes open. The Prime Minister hasn't appeared in public for a month now. He hasn't been to the Salon for almost two months because his man there died."

"One of the artisans?"

"Hit by a tram. It was a terrible mess. The Prime Minister has never used anyone else. You're the blessing he's been waiting for."

What dwelled inside this boy that so outlandish a plan could be hatched in him? What had the rebels promised him? Was it simply power, or the possibility of it? I imagined him, these last months, by the fires up in the hills. Perhaps it was *he* who sang, his pure tenor floating on the evening air, coming down to me so diminished I still doubted that I'd ever heard it.

And what had he to do with "her," Lucrezia, she whose song was sung so passionately each evening, as if in church? How could one so young ever truly understand the powers of her voice? There was the key, the link to Lucrezia, that turned in the center of me to lock or unlock any commitment I might make to this cause. Surely I would say yes to him, though I had no idea yet what I meant by it. To what was I saying yes?

"I can help you," I whispered, "but you'll have to be with me."

"I will," he agreed.

"Because I still have no idea what I'm doing."

"It's all very simple. You'll not have to do anything out of the ordinary."

"Just my normal work? No interrogations?"

"None at all. You must be just what he expects. A little dull, steady. We need him to trust you."

I could not keep from staring. "I can't believe that it's you. You still seem like a movie to me." He took my hand and let the blanket drop from his shoulders into his lap. And then he pressed my fingers to his skin, there beside the sternum where his heart beat. I felt it, pulsing beneath his bones, and I felt the warm flat of his chest and the soft nipple.

"It's me," he whispered. "Believe it."

And then, when we slept, it was as if afloat in a black, endless sea. The waves cradled me gently with no shoreline in evidence and the horizon, too, impossibly absent, for the sky and sea were one substance. I did not dream, or if I did it was forgotten in the gray light of late morning. I awoke to find the little nest of blankets where the boy had slept empty. I couldn't remember any disturbance, any noise or rustling in the night. His clothes were gone too, all except a long strip of his bandanna that he had torn off and left hanging by my coat. There was a note, stuffed into my pocket.

"Mr. Sludge," it began. "Do not worry about me. I'll return within a few days, at night. Until that time I remain yours with faith, Hakan." Hakan. What a beautiful, exotic name. It suited him, I thought, to sign his name, to not remain anonymous. He was so young and full of reckless confidence. He could have devised no more vigorous and innocent an affirmation of our bond than the signing of his lovely name.

I stared at the few words for some time, mimicking the movement of his childish hand with mine. Had he written against the wall, almost forgetting, in his haste, to leave any note? I scanned the dull white surface for any impression he might have made. There was nothing.

My clothing was stiff from the heater, and I put it in the closet and went to fill the tub for my morning bath. Today would be busy, with a visit to the laboratory of Flessinger and Ponz, followed in the late afternoon by my Doctor-General. I was supposed to spend the few idle hours writing, but I had no intention of doing that. My life had turned fully forward, off that brief and frustrating path. The small shred of cloth he'd left me was a blessed thing, a tiny sacrament I'd keep pressed to my bosom for all but the half-hour I spent in the tub. It still smelled of him, of "Hakan" and his sweat.

A bank of weather now covered the city. The architecture of the old district pressed silently against the sky. To the north, along the clean-swept Avenue of Progress, the regimented palaces of the ministries sat like stones, stacked in long flat rows facing the sea. Like the ministers themselves, the buildings were kept up and not allowed to age. They sported only those marks of time the architects planned into the original design—a certain type of marble, scored with gravel and acid, say; a false exterior stair which crumbles at its top. The building is frozen in the moment of its birth. They are all kept this way or torn down.

Regardless, the snow fell, leaving its heavy mantle on the copper roofs of the old district and the long stone lines of the Avenue of Progress. I opened my windows to let the chilly moistness in, a startling, bracing breeze across my bare skin. The bath was raising a fine steam, billowing across the black and white tiles, and I set the tea water to boil upon the stove. It seemed a good morning to visit the fish vendor, to have my breakfast fresh, and I did so right away.

I walked with a different aspect that morning. To have met (and become?) a rebel, the opposition, elevated me in my own eyes above the mass. The tattered bandanna hung loosely against my chest, hidden by my garments. Beneath it my heart beat a loud tattoo. It was not the color or meaning of the vestment that made my blood race so, it was the smell of it, his smell.

Could anyone guess? By looking into my eyes, say, could the tricolors be read there? Was it possible to detect the sudden and complete change I had undergone in the darkest hours of the night? No. The thought of it thrilled me. I was, to all appearances, just what I had been, yesterday and every day before ... But it wasn't so; I had changed, was now "the opposition." Surely no greater change was possible—yet it could not be seen. The fishmonger carried out his business precisely as he always had. The little boy by the news vendors said a cheery hello, receiving his hard candy with the usual polite enthusiasm. The tram conductor gave me the customary nod of the head and said nothing. I pressed my hand to my breast, feeling the slight protrusion that said it was indeed true. How many more aboard this tram harbored the same secret?

Snow piled high on either side of the bare metal tracks, pushed there by the workmen with their shovels. I watched the crowd exiting at my stop and wondered which of them might be technicians, or which engaged in some capacity with the course of my therapy. I was clueless. The functionaries offered no outward sign of their specializations. They all wore the light blue hats of the city's sports teams. I ducked under the stone steps and rang for Flessinger and Ponz.

It was so welcoming, the laboratory and its anteroom. A box had been laid out for me and I filled it, stripping quickly in the warmth of the carpeted room. My gown slipped neatly on, I proceeded to the main room and the chair itself. No one was in evidence. The dim lights of the window box did not flicker; no shadows passed before them. I had never encountered the lab empty, but it didn't trouble me. This was as much my home, by now, as theirs. I sat down and waited. The screen, too, was idle. It hung dirty and creased in the bright light. (Odd that when struck by a particular light, that cast by the projector, it should disappear so cleanly into its function.)

The lights went out. Then the booth was busy with activity; burly men of unfamiliar size and shape bustled about in the soft darkness.

"Hello," I called, quite loudly. "I'm not ready. I've not been strapped in yet." My cries weren't heard. Evidently the intercom had not been turned on. The screen filled with light, yellow at first and then orange. I watched from my chair, instinctively loosening the gown, as the screen went black again and the leader ran with its telltale green scratches. Of course I expected the boy, Hakan, my heart racing at the prospect. I could feel his face near to mine, and clutched my chest, reaching for that one scrap of him, the bandanna, but I'd left it with my clothes.

A little girl appeared, and a dog. It was a film I'd never seen. The dog had syringes dangling from his scruffy back, ending in thin, flexible tubes running from one into the next. It was some sort of exterior circulatory system and seemed to contain blood. The little girl was naked. Her head had been shaved and she was groggy. The dog was coming near her and she seemed about to fall over, when suddenly the image disappeared under another, projected from a second, more powerful, machine.

Wind began coursing through the chamber. A few dozen old men were sprawled across one another on a thick shag carpet. Their faces looked familiar, but the camera never focused long enough for me to place them. They were naked, and many of them were bald. An awful sound came from the screen, the various squishings and fartings of sweaty flesh, as they pressed against one another. I recognized my minister, the future Wilderness head, groping near the camera. He was faceless (which is to say I saw his real face) and seemed about to come.

The film disappeared and it began to rain. Fresh drops pelted the open room, brisk as a spring shower, and I pulled my gown up over my head, huddling in the chair. The screen was hit by a rapid montage of images, pretty paintings, naked children, mug shots, muscled men, helmeted technicians, scientific teams inspecting fissures, buildings on fire, rippled torsos, gleaming race cars, literally hundreds of towers, and as many buxom ladies, succeeding one another like so many torn pages. Surely they couldn't calibrate a meaningful response at this speed? And then the fumes began, and the chair started to shake in a manner of which I'd never known it capable. I leaped up and hurried to the black window, banged on it with my fist, and shouted to the men to stop.

"I'm not ready," I said through the glass. "I have no phallometer on." Some of my message got through. Switches were thrown or levers pressed, ending the sudden storm. Lights came on in both enclosures. A short man with a tag reading "Marketing Research" took charge and approached me.

"Just who," he asked in an angry voice, "do you think you are?"

"I'm sorry, they've instructed me to remain anonymous."

"Who? *Who* has instructed you?" He gestured to the men in the booth, making little dialing motions with his hand.

"My Doctor-General said I may not give my real name, as it may imperil the objectivity of my treatment."

"You're a patient, then."

"Of sorts."

"Of sorts, I see. And who *is* your Doctor-General, pray tell?" What a silly question. Everyone knew that our city was blessed with but one Doctor-General, the Mr. D. G. Nicholas Nicholas.

"Why, Doctor-General Nicholas Nicholas, of course. And he'll be quite upset when he hears word of this unprovoked malpractice. I'd be surprised if some heads did not roll." I was dripping wet in my flimsy gown.

And then two burly men entered, led by the duo of my daily

treatments, Flessinger and Ponz. "Oh, at last." I swooned with not undue drama. "Just look at me."

The poor little man with the marketing tag was taken to task right then and there, drawn across the carpet, brought down and cut up, by the justly incensed Flessinger The others were sent scattering, looking for towels and my dry clothes while Flessinger began his apology.

"Mr. uh, uh, we are terribly sorry. The equipment is occasionally run full speed, you see. Test marketing, saturation advertising, and all that . . . though I cannot imagine why the door was not properly closed, or the room checked, as is standard procedure. You can be sure this will not go unnoticed."

"I should hope not. I was just settling in, as you can imagine . . . letting my gown loose and all."

"But why weren't you told about the changes?"

"Changes?"

"Your lab sessions are being curtailed. That's why we had no one here to greet you."

"I'm to have no more films?" I asked, alarmed at the prospect. The fawning technicians returned with my clothes, each one clutching an item like some holy reliquary.

"No more. You're being moved to a different therapy."

"But that can't be." It meant I'd never see Hakan on film again. "I demand an explanation."

"I cannot give one," the calm little pill replied.

"But surely a man has rights, even within the Criminal and Health systems. You can't get away with this." I was bundled into my garments by the attendants, and piece by piece slipped back into my dry costume.

"I'm afraid it's up to the Doctor-General. He's ordered it, and only he can give you an explanation."

"Will there be films with the new therapy, or slides at least?"

"I don't believe so."

"And to exactly where, Mr. Flessinger, shall I report for the mysterious new procedure?" I had so looked forward to a morning of films and fumes, powerful shocks and the chance to see Hakan again through fresh eyes.

"It's quite nearby, really. You haven't far to go."

It had begun to snow again. A big ship crossed the harbor, heading out into the storm. Its black metal hull rode low in the swollen waters, the hold burdened by the product of our factories. Foam slapped off the waves and froze with the snow against it. What sailors rode this ship? I could see a handful buried in thick parkas, their faces hidden behind fur lining. They held fast to whatever the ship would offer, thin metal railings, crusted with ice, vents and valves of enormous height and girth (a wonder no one fell straight in one), and each other, struggling against the wind to share a cigarette or conversation.

It was their view, their perspective on the city, that I envied. The ocean offered a certain opportunity for distance and mobility. Each feature of our city took its place in the progress of shapes and panoramas such a gradual leave-taking afforded. The slow pulling away, our city resolved into ever new and different formations ... each degree of distance creates a new frame within which to view it. Was there a final frame? Could one, in the end, somewhere beyond the impossible heavens, leave the final frame and float, unenclosed, above it all? (Another question for philosophers.) And where had Hakan come from?

Being so near, I took time to walk east, away from the seawall, toward the valley of the gray factories. I had not visited since my stroll several weeks before, and I thought it would be nice to see the ruins under snow. The flat valley opened up as if onto another century. Small houses sat along empty, narrow streets where no mark had been left by the plows. Smoke came from the black metal pipes which graced the houses. Beyond them, the factories rose like a wall, shrouded in a veil of white, and I walked toward them through the storm.

The cisterns, where the tall stacks had collapsed, were frozen thick with ice. I held the broken wire fence down with my foot and climbed across. The Ministry had plans to make the old factory into an art museum. I stepped carefully across the fallen bricks, letting them shift and settle under me. The main building, still standing, was pitted and scarred by the collapse of the stacks. It was graced by three wide arches through which the trains used to pass. I walked under the central arch and into the great hall. In the heyday of this factory, trains came three abreast to be loaded and sent north; more trains followed, as close as the signalmen would allow. Snow came through the ash-blackened beams where the roof was torn off. What floor there was had long ago rotted or sunk, leaving only mud and dirt. The arches opened up on all sides, letting the storm blow both inside and out. In church, a similar silence reigned. But the arches there framed views of heaven and the saints, locked in stained glass.

The wind blew through the bare, burned lattice, into the open sky. In church, incense burned where no wind could put it out. The church was shut tight, while the ruin was laid open, raw like a surgical wound. Soon they would plug it shut, fill the empty archways, scrub the bricks clean and put a roof on, to make it suitable for the presentation of art.

I passed from the great hall into a labyrinth of broken machines. Why should fallen brick move me? The fact of its failure to enclose started a warmth behind my eyes, a ticklish feeling. The ruin displayed itself nakedly; it showed its long, slow decline, its simple failure to stand against time and the weather.

The littered dirt stretched from where I stood and stopped,

exactly where the line of brick still stood . . . and yet it stretched beyond, under rubble and away, visible through the arches. The air extended upward, toward the line of wooden beams, burned and sagging above . . . and went on, exceeding the boundary of the room. It was in that pause, that slight holding of breath upon reaching the boundary, that I felt my sadness well up inside. It rolled from below my heart, caught for a moment in the persistence and failure of the walls to hold. I felt it push at my eyes. I saw a hundred faces, absurd constructions draped ambitiously over bones, meant to function as shields of some sort, boundaries or masks, protecting an elusive thing inside, and yet failing, finally, to mask anything at all. There was no inside or outside; the air passed easily through, in breath and words.

This was something of a crisis for me. The sadness seemed at once sacred and overblown. Its roots remained obscure and inaccessible. The gasping of my mouth, as I stood there among the bricks, while, to all appearances, simply a feature of my crying, felt actually like the workings of a mouth wanting words which went unfound. It ended only by my growing tired and walking south, out of the ruins, through the factory yard and, finally, to home.

I had my appointment to consider, and a good deal on my mind. I thought it best to stop at home and freshen up before going to see my Doctor-General. It was clear I would not mention most of what had transpired in the last twenty-four hours. What a treacherous thing the city had become. I boarded a southbound tram and kept my head buried in the day's newspaper. The very walls harbored such disturbing ghosts and ideas. I could not risk looking up at them. There had settled on them a brittleness and fragility, as if they might shatter under my eyes. My own face bothered me, and I couldn't help picking at it, scratching at a small sore that threatened to unravel. Happily, no one sat near me. I'd never felt so eager to flee into our inner sanctum and pull the sacred bag down over my head.

"Prompt, as usual," my cheery Doctor-General said when I arrived. "I'd thought the storm might delay you." He had his magnifying glass strapped on and was bent over an osprey, or some other kind of bird. He did not notice my agitation, nor the slight bleeding of my sore.

"Oh, no," I sighed, trying to keep an even voice. "The trams are all up and running." A swift incision with his knife told me he was in no hurry to get started. The osprey squirmed and buckled in its harness, mute and unsedated. "May I just wait inside, Doctor, please," I enjoined. "With my bag?"

He paused in his work and looked up. His face showed warm concern despite its spatterings of blood. "Anxious, are we? I won't be a minute."

"I'll just go ahead then?"

"Yes, do." He relaxed his grasp on the animal's neck and turned back to the small tray of instruments. I beat my retreat with haste, letting the heavy door seal shut behind me. The bag slipped on like a dream.

Then, the rustle of his clothes, softly dropping off him . . . I lay quietly, waiting for his word. Silence, and then:

"What are you thinking?"

"You," I answered. "You and your selfless work, your health. I worry sometimes." There was the sparkling image of the Doctor-General. It was more of a burden than most men had, and I knew him well enough now to see its poor fit.

"What do you worry about?"

"Your face, sometimes, fearing that it might collapse. Isn't it hard, keeping it up so?" How often I'd imagined him, returning from his work, the hour hideously late. Passing the opera house he glances up the Fish Street and sees the low cellar doorway. I know he cannot go there; he risks everything if he does. And what about the awful prospect of censure for his unorthodox methods, and the animals. "If your colleagues can't see fit to support your work," I counseled, "I'm worried you'll just give it up and have some sort of breakdown."

"My, uh, surgical investigations?"

"Yes, especially that. Isn't it awfully trying? Don't you sometimes just want to go home and peel that face off, just not be the Doctor-General anymore?"

"What would you do?"

"If I were the Doctor-General?"

"If you had the urge to peel your face off."

"I didn't say *I* had that urge. Please stop trying to change the subject." I lay still in my bag, fumbling with a few thoughts, wishing for some greater bond than the one we'd so carefully forged. I knew he feared it, just as he had feared my mention of Lucrezia.

"I wasn't trying to change the subject."

"Well, you certainly had that effect." Why did he deflect me? It was, perhaps, his training. Schooled in the techniques of self-effacement he instinctively disappeared whenever my interests turned his way. He was like my shadow, cast by some light strapped on my body. Each time I turned to look he'd disappear.

"Why do you think I am evading?" He whispered uncomfortably while shifting in his chair. His pencil wasn't tacking. I lay and listened keenly as he rustled about in the corner.

"You're not getting dressed, are you?" I asked.

"Well, I, it's quite chilly in here." Scoundrel. I'd caught him at it.

"I'm shocked, Doctor. First the little miscue with Flessinger, and now you're sneaking into your clothes while my back is turned."

"Miscue with Flessinger?"

"You were supposed to inform me of certain changes in my aversive therapy. I'd hardly think to mention it if it weren't for your unpleasant conduct today, in the inner chamber no less."

"Oh lord, yes. I . . . there's no excuse. I've just had no time, what with the municipal cadavers. I'm making such progress, you see." I heard contrition in his voice.

"Yes, yes you are. And no one recognizes it."

"Absolutely, no one. They avoid me like the plague."

"Oh, but they'll see."

"If only they knew what I'm on the verge of, the great leap forward."

"The knife."

"Oh yes, the knife. To cut it out. I'm almost able now to cut it out. Why, you saw the osprey in the anteroom? What passivity, what grace and calm, without anesthetic, mind you. I've only a few steps to go before I can be sure, God willing."

"Yet your busy life stops you."

"Oh, at every turn."

"Though you'd like to."

"Would I, and just for a few weeks, two months perhaps, to develop my technique. We're a lifetime away from perfecting it, of course, but at last I'm ready to begin."

"Yes. You'll not leave me, will you?" I could hold back my selfish concerns no longer.

"Leave you? Why, we're just getting to the good stuff, after all. Your sores are, I believe, about to open up and blossom."

"My sores, Doctor?"

"Your psychic wounds."

"Is that the impetus behind my new aversive treatments?"

"Well, yes, partly. The, uh, progress with your earlier treatments had, had gone as far as it could. We'd like to step it up a notch."

"More films?"

"Well, no more films actually."

"Tapes?"

"You will be continuing with the tapes, yes."

"And?"

"We've secured a coach for you, the best."

"A coach?"

"Yes, you'll know him simply as 'Coach.' Covert sensitization. It's one of these 'imaginary aversive therapies.'"

"You mean, it doesn't actually happen?"

"Oh no, no. Of course it actually happens, that is, the therapy itself does take place. The uh, incidents are, however, imaginary. You run through them in your head, you see, or out loud, with the coach."

"I recite fantasies to the coach?"

"Or he to you, I'm not exactly clear on it."

"Will I be strapped in, you know, to the device?"

"Oh yeah, you bet."

"I begin tomorrow?"

"Tomorrow morning, I believe. And again on Friday." The coach was not entirely welcome. I had no wish to be bounced from laboratory to laboratory, functioning as fodder for experimental therapies throughout the Ministry.

"Couldn't *we* just recite fantasies to one another, my Doctor-General? Here, in our sanctorum?"

"I'm afraid I couldn't. I don't have the same extensive training as the coach. These therapies aren't simple toys to be played with by amateurs."

I left the ministerial building wallowing in a dull euphoria. I'd become a rebel with Hakan, confidante to my Doctor-General, rumored manicurist to the Prime Minister, cast-off failure of

Flessinger and Ponz, future victim of the as yet unknown coach, and all in the space of less than a day (not to mention my disturbing episode in the ruins). I was a party to which everyone had suddenly come, and being the party itself, I could not simply step out for some fresh air. How I wished to have been on that heavy ship that sailed to sea in the morning, burdened by some simple task, peeling the potatoes, say. An evening alone at the Eichelberger seemed like a good idea. I went there posthaste, stopping at the news kiosk along the way.

I opened the paper and slipped inside it, hoping I might somehow disappear, awash in the municipal news. There was ample analysis of the storm and its effect on our economy and spirit. Traditionally our Prime Minister welcomed the first snows with the Winter Proclamation, a spirited affirmation of the values of hoarding and thrift. But this year the ritual had been mysteriously forgone (thus bolstering the fantastic claims of Hakan concerning the Prime Minister's face). What an awful mess if he'd had no upkeep in over two months. But that got me back to me. I flipped forward to the pageants. The proprietress, Miss Eichelberger, descended, hovering close by with a complimentary liqueur, a thick opalescent green pool wobbling deep inside a brandy snifter.

"Thank you very much," I said politely. "What is it?" Normally I didn't drink aperitifs, but my impenetrable hostess stood by expectantly, offering not a clue as to the nature and composition of her gift. Her posture and delicate brow told me "Drink it," so I did. It tasted of mint and Chartreuse, a heady, intoxicating brew that slipped sweetly down my throat.

"Like it?" she asked in her deep baritone, taking the broad glass in hand and licking it. She waddled back toward the kitchen to fetch some more. I enjoyed these small privileges quite a bit. They marked me as someone special within the confines of the small café, a regular, an insider and confidante of the mistress.

My minister was in the newspaper, his lion-sized jaws jutting powerfully toward the cameras. He was seen mending fences in the municipal woodlands, having walked out through the snows on foot (accompanied, one must think, by a few score of photographers and print journalists). It was nice to see his dog again, and of course the familiar walking stick. Preparations were under way for the Festival of the Snows, sponsored by the university. It was a junior pageant of sorts, an opportunity for students to set up and execute an event similar in style and scope to the real thing. There would be the usual presentations, the dignitarial dais organized minutely, an instructive tableau of faces and figures, and, of course, an orchestra. The impious students could never resist some mild irreverence. Last year a man sporting the Prime Minister's face had appeared on the dais with a prosthetic penis hanging where his nose should be.

The storm had abated. A few tiny flakes floated in the air, blown from the ground and off roofs by the occasional push of wind. The café was warm. I quaffed the long train of liqueurs and nibbled at my meal. The cares of the day gradually dissolved and I finished the evening quite late, nursing a black coffee. Walking back, crunching through the day's fresh drifts, I passed close by the Burlesque and could not keep myself from going in. I wasn't home until morning.

The coach's "quarters," "crypt," "crèche," or "bower," as he variously called the room where we met, was not at all like the laboratory of Flessinger and Ponz. Where the latter chamber had been bare and subterranean, the coach occupied a cramped garret in the far reaches of the ministerial attic. As one faces the edifice there is visible a steep copper topping plate, running along the upper edge of the palace. It is two stories in height, and only occasionally punctuated by a window or vent of some sort. Behind this metal decoration a series of tiny rooms was carved out of the storage space, and one of these belonged to the coach. He'd left a note on the door which bade me undress and secure the device while I waited. Most unorthodox, I thought, to have me secure it on my own, without supervision. Happily I knew how, having watched the technicians perform this same task for me.

I glanced around the little room, looking for the telltale knobs and nozzles that might give me some glimpse of the coach's methods. There was little, only stacks of dull medical books and one small screen of meters set directly in front of me. The little needles were at rest, languishing in their leftmost positions. Through a tiny window to my right I could see a bit of the harbor and the occasional bird, and that was my only distraction. I sniffed, shifting in my chair, and waited.

It was quite some time before his footsteps approached, echoing along the empty hallway outside. The door banged open and shut with a violent suddenness and the coach quickly barked his first command, that I was not to turn and look at him.

"The needles. Watch the needles."

I looked there. Indeed the hair-thin needles had begun dancing, shifting lightly across their scales, responding to even this slight excitement in my penis. It was an electronic wonder, more sensitive to my arousal than even I.

"I want you to think of a boy, a delicious, beautiful boy," the coach began without introductions or a warning of any sort. "He's in his underpants, standing by a little rug." This was not so bad. "Do you see him? Tell me, do you see him?"

"Yes," I shouted back, easily catching the spirit of this unusual exchange. "Yes, I see him, tall, lanky, his . . . "

"His underpants are stirring, yes, that's right, sir. The tall, lanky, nearly nude boy's underpants are stirring. Can you see them, are you near enough to see them? Tell me."

"Oh yes, yes. Why, I'm almost breathing on them, I . . ."

"And can you see the needles, are the needles dancing?"

"Why, yes, they are, in fact. They're dancing up and down, like my beating heart."

"And your face is so near to his belly you can taste him, taste his sweet brown skin."

"Yes, it is."

"Your tongue has nearly slipped in under the elastic waistband."

"Yes, yes it has."

"Your breath across his skin."

"Oh yes."

"Now vomit, sir! Puke all over him! Spit it up, choking bilious vomit all down over his front. Are you doing it?"

"Sickness?"

"Puke it out, coughing, noxious barf splattered all over him."

"Well, I . . ."

"Spit up, my friend, spit up I say. Upchuck your guts and stain him, dirty, stinking boy."

"How awful."

"Awful boy, yes, awful he is, and run away, run away from him now. Run, run, sir."

"Run away?"

"Swiftly, like the wind. Run, run away, run away." My enthusiastic coach paused for a moment, catching his breath. "Are the needles coming down? Have you brought them down?"

"I, yes."

"Further. Bring them down till they drop, ugly boy. Your bile and barf is dripping down him, stinging the open sores of his pussy zits. Red, and bursting, stinging pain, isn't it so? Say it's so."

"Oh my."

"His shriveled little prick hidden in the sputum, it stinks of shit. Shit, don't you know it?"

"I, no."

"And his thin legs buckle under as he faints from the stink, falling in his own feces. Have you run, sir, have you run away?"

"I, yes."

"Yes, yes, you have run away, and you detest this boy, you hate and revile him, stinking, ugly, bad boy, bad, bad boy."

"How awful."

"Are the needles down, sir, are they at last down?"

"Down completely."

He heaved a deep and satisfied sigh. "Congratulations, you're gonna beat this thing, I know it. Shall we have another go?"

And so we did, nine or ten goes in all before the coach's prodigious energies were spent and we stopped to take a breather. I certainly did *not* love it (as my increasingly fallible Doctor-General had assured me I would). In the unlikely event that I might reach orgasm, the coach told me, we'd not even bother replacing the bag, leaving me, instead, all shriveled inside the cold, clammy goo. It was barbaric, medieval, when compared to the pleasant methods of Flessinger and Ponz.

That afternoon it happened. Hakan's prophecy came true. Doctor Cotton had called imploring me to be prompt. He did not divulge the reason for the uncharacteristic reminder. I became nervous as a schoolgirl thinking of him, the Prime Minister, and the costume I would wear. Since the evening of the boy's daring prediction I'd kept a freshly washed smock and nylon hair net (together with one of Doctor Cotton's surgical masks) in a canvas bag beside my bed. An artisan to the Prime Minister should be clean, circumspect, spotless. Had I ever doubted the boy? The well-creased smock said I had not. It wasn't surprise I felt then at the call, so much as vertigo. I packed the clean outfit together with my tools and set off to my rendezvous.

The Salon door had been shoveled clear of snow and I stood on the wet steps and rang. How annoying that crooked little man was, he whom Doctor Cotton had retained and whose primary function was the opening of the door. I could hear him scraping along the hallway at a snail's pace, chatting even with my colleagues while I waited in the snow. I couldn't imagine that our clients would ever put up with such treatment and wondered if, perhaps, there was some signal they used to prod him, some secret rhythm of ringing that let him know a VIP was outside waiting. I simply leaned on the buzzer without surcease until the door swung, finally, open.

"Mr. Adjutant," I bade curtly, stepping past him and into the hallway. I marched straight to the chair and pulled the polishing rag from its place. The whole apparatus was in need of a good overhaul, but there wasn't enough time for that. I sprayed some dissolving agent on the blood splatters and let it soak in a bit. A wad of fish skin had been wedged into the seat, obviously stuffed there in haste. This was too much.

"Ah, Mr. Sludge," the melodious Doctor Cotton crooned, spotting me from the door of his office. "What on earth are you doing?"

"I'm cleaning my station of course, Doctor. I'm on at noon, as you know." I held the bloody rag up as evidence.

"But you'll not be at your station today." His tone said I was stupid. "Didn't my adjutant tell you?"

"Mr. Adjutant?" I asked back, squinching my nose. "Why, he barely managed to open the door for me." Doctor Cotton came close.

"You'll be working in the Chamber today."

"He requires the Chamber?" My colleague's alarm said I'd, perhaps, spilled the beans.

"You're familiar with this client?"

"I . . . I've had a certain feeling since your call."

"Well, then." Doctor Cotton nodded, scribbling a note onto his pad. "He requires privacy, and circumspection. I suggest you get your tools and wait in the Chamber. You are to leave the lights off until he instructs you otherwise. Is that clear?"

"Oh yes, Doctor. Is there anything else, anything special I should do?"

"Simply treat him with the usual tact and deference we show to our clients."

"Yes, I certainly will."

"I know you will. That's why you've been recommended to this man. I think you'll find him very pleasant and agreeable." I hurried to the cluttered lockers, pulling my clean gown and hair net from the bag.

It was silent in the lightless Chamber. I stood still and pulled a dull green surgical mask on, feeling its long strings with both hands. I reached blindly behind my head to fasten them. The fit was good. My nose was untrammeled, my breathing easy. My eyes took on a wise, fugitive air, as though they were spies darting out above their hiding place. I felt I might at any moment duck entirely behind the cloth and hide out there. The door came slowly open, and a solitary man walked in unannounced.

He was steady and unhurried. Closing the door behind him, he stood in the dark with me, not reaching for the lights or extending a word or hand in greeting. I listened as he slipped his greatcoat off and laid it by the door. I would have felt awkward if not for the sedative calm that seemed to emanate from him and fill the room. He shuffled near, feeling blindly, and touched me, as if by accident, on his way to the chair. He settled there.

"You are Mr. Sludge?" he asked in a worn and tired voice.

"Yes, yes I am."

"Good. Very good." The fact seemed to lift a weight from him. "You've probably a fair idea who I am, though you have the good breeding and tact not to have made an issue of it."

"Thank you, sir. It needn't be an issue."

"Very good. You recommend yourself well." I felt his cold hand grubbing at my gown, clutching and pulling at its fabric. He worked his way across my thigh and onto my hip.

"Sir?"

"Your hand, Mr. Sludge, I wish to take your hand."

"Very well." I took his four fingers into my grip, cupping the whole hand in mine. It was a frail, ancient thing, crossed by lumpy veins and swollen joints, its leatherish skin pulled taut along his thin fingers. It trembled as I held it, the pulse palpable along every line.

"I'm quite old now. You've noticed that."

"Yes, I have."

"My body doesn't work so well, my hands. You can feel them, can't you?"

"Yes, I can."

"I don't suppose you'll recognize me when we turn the lights on. No one recognizes me." He stopped, lost, I supposed, in the implications of this thought. He wanted no response. "It's quite ironic. Though I have come to value the small freedoms it grants me, the anonymity."

The Prime Minister chuckled at some private thought. I stood still, holding his hand more tenderly now. It had warmed some, and seemed to steady as his spirits rose.

"I think, Mr. Sludge, sometimes . . . I say, I sometimes think I'm the only man in the government who doesn't look like me."

His hand pulled away from mine and the chair shook, racked by his spasm of coughing and laughter as he was overcome by this small joke. "Get me some water, would you please?" His throat rattled with phlegm. I felt my way around the countertop, searching for the cold steel faucet.

There was no cup and I told him so. He could only cough in reply, his body banging against the chair. I turned the faucet on, letting it run a moment, and cupped my hands underneath, filling them with the cold water.

"I have the water in my hands, sir." He let his breathing go shallow for a moment, and guided me toward his mouth. The Prime Minister drank from my hands like a beggar child, impatient and grateful, then licked the last drops with his tongue.

"Much better." He whispered, his throat still rough and occluded. "At least I have my voice back." He patted my damp hands. "Sit," he ordered. I pulled the technician's stool closer, resisting an urge to touch his face. I wished that I were able to work in the dark, so that our intimacy would never be disturbed by the violence of the lights. The cool water dried from my hands; the world was blocked from us by the heavy door. I was floating, my mind loosed from my body in a moment not unlike my occasional ecstatic delirium ... though now I felt more submerged than afloat, anchored to the frail old man lying next to me.

"It's quite comfortable, the dark." His voice filled it, a disembodied whisper. "If I could write and read in it, I think I might never turn the lights on."

"I wish I could do my work in it."

"Yes, that would be fine, wouldn't it," he agreed. "But of course you can't."

"No, I can't." The Prime Minister took my hand again and pressed it in among the folds of his shirt.

"You can feel my heart?" he asked tenderly. "It's very strong, isn't it?" I did feel it, the patient muscle swelling and collapsing by the bony sternum. It was strong, and even, continuing the work it had begun at some mysterious, unplaceable moment inside his mother's womb. Some moment *before* him, when cells became tissue and moved together, powering a pulse. It pulsed through the morning of his birth, when he was first brought out into the light and violence of the world; it marked a rhythm through childhood afternoons, and raced through the days of adolescence, seeming to sink in sadness and rise in times of jubilation. Now, lying in the chair—uncertain of what he had become— the Prime Minister pushed his frail hand inside his shirt, with mine, to feel the muscle work. I pressed my fingers to his chest, enchanted.

"Yes, it is strong, very strong," I said.

"Remember that, please. Remember *that* when you see me."

I cannot describe the sight, when the lights came on. I began with a small desk lamp by the wall. Its position was unfortunate; it cast ghastly shadows across the folded, cratered mix of failed prosthetics and flesh. His attempt at a smile was hideous, transformed into a hysterical, leering gash. I averted my gaze, moving to the counter to prepare my tools.

"Tell me when your eyes have adjusted," I asked him, glad I'd worn a mask behind which I could hide my reactions. "Then I'll get the overhead lights." He lay there in silence. He had no control over the message and effect of his face. Hopelessly, he tried the animated ticks and contractions of muscle that, at one time, resulted in smiles and winks, archings of the brow and winsome glances. Now they produced chaos, the tangled remains of his mask transforming them into grotesques, unpatterned swellings and collapsings that coursed across his face like ocean waves.

"I'm quite adjusted now," he allowed, signaling me to bring

the bright lights on. His voice, at least, was still steady and controlled. I resolved to focus my attention there. His face would be nothing more than an object, a broken thing in need of repair. I pushed the two heavy buttons by the door, bringing the overhead lights to life. The brightness improved things, or I had gotten used to him. In either case, it was better now. The sight of him did not move me to pity and revulsion, as it had at first.

"Well, well," I remarked cheerfully. "We've got quite the job ahead of us."

"I suspect so," he answered. "Not that I expect any miracles."

"I can give you any face you wish, without miracles." I began poking at what lay before me, trying to determine what of it was flesh and what putty.

"Well, I'll only be needing my old face," he offered. "The one I had last year. Surely you're familiar with it." I'd seen it often, in the papers and on billboards. It still graced many of the banners and insignia, enjoying a longevity that many thought an inspired gesture affirming the stability of the Prime Minister and his ideas . . . in fact, I knew now, its roots were quite other than that.

"I'll need some good photos," I said. "Both profiles and one shot from the front."

"I'll have them sent."

"And some time. I'll have to excavate your real face before I can set up the new one. No use building on this foundation."

"What do you mean, my real face?"

"The one you had originally, before any of the remodeling."

"But that's so long ago, I, I can't imagine it's still there."

"Don't be silly, of course it is. And probably in good tone too, protected from the weather and all."

"Will I have aged, do you think?"

"Yes, though the skin, as I say, should be quite young. Protected from the sun, you see."

"I see. Is this a difficult or painful procedure?"

"No, no. Not if I take the time to do it properly."

"And how long is that?"

"Well, things are quite a mess. I may need a week or two just to find the original face. Maybe another week or two, then, to clean it up. We can't rush this part if you want a decent reconstruction."

"A month?"

"More; that's simply the first stage."

"Could you have me ready for the first thaw?"

"March?"

"Perhaps even February, I'm told. Global warming, you know. I've got to be ready for the Melting Pageant."

"Well." I knew it was possible, if everything went smoothly. "Consider it done. You have my word on it."

THE PROSPECT OF THIS LONG ORDEAL THUS DEFINED MY WINTER. Many more important changes would come to pass in those months, but I viewed them then, and look back on them now, in their relation to the Prime Minister's face. That was the week his nose came clean, I might remark when remembering the evening Hakan, slightly drunk, at last kissed me with his honey lips. The collapse of his chin that day had put me in a funk, I'd think, searching for a reason why I'd been so short-tempered with the coach. It gave my days a regularity and purpose I'd not known since forced out of teaching, imbuing me with a calm and dignity that even my Doctor-General took time to note.

"You're much less anxious lately," he observed correctly, one evening in the outer chamber, where such wild speculations were fair game. "Is your writing going particularly well?" I can't blame the poor guess on him, really. I'd misled him consistently on this score, finding in "writing" a handy metaphor for my project with the Prime Minister.

I found it impossible to keep from discussing my new work (though I knew it to be far outside the bounds of good health in this my new life). So I fashioned a conceit by which I might share my triumph with the Doctor-General. *The Prime Minister's Face* was a book I was writing, or so I told him. I'd begun with two weeks or so of stripping away the "false presumptions," searching for the structure and foundation of the story. Having found the "natural structure," I spent another two weeks cleaning it up (certain extensions, right in the middle, turned out to be wrong, not at all part of the "bare bones" from which I wanted to work). I then began "fleshing out" the story, working alternately on its various sections. I hoped to get a workable draft within a month. Then revisions would begin.

By this conceit I was able to discuss the trials and tribulations, the small victories and technical challenges presented to me by *The Prime Minister's Face* without dragging the Doctor-General into an ugly dilemma (easily the equal of the Lucrezia debacle I'd precipitated only a few short weeks earlier). It was in the period of "cleaning up" (week four of my work) that my counselor offered his generous assessment of my mental health and asked how my writing might have contributed to it.

"Remarkable progress," I told him. "Just today I found a good balance between the top and bottom. I'd thought it was going to be so heady you know, all high-forehead stuff. But really it's not. Got to have more from the mouth . . . dialogue, you see. Quite symmetrical now that I've gotten a clear view."

"Well, it all sounds remarkable. I've never pretended to understand artists, mind you, all those arcane, abstract concerns. Give me a good cadaver any day."

"It's really quite the same challenge," I assured him. "Structure, digging for clues, and all."

"I guess so, though a cadaver is much more unyielding than a story. You can't just, uh, reimagine it."

"No, no," I hastened to correct him. "Nor can you 'just reimagine' a story. It shares with the cadaver a stubbornness, a shape and feel with which the artist must not tamper. I've not the ease you have at discovering it, mind you. I can't pull it out on its frozen tray and simply measure it. I spend long days sifting it carefully through my fingers, so to speak, my mind . . . separating the true from the false materials, getting down to what really belongs there."

"Yes, I see. Ultimately the writer must write the story that is true, that somehow fits."

"And reinvigorate it by his embellishments, thus fiction, you see."

"Yes, fiction," my Doctor-General repeated absently. Reaching toward me with warm arms, he took me by my shoulders. "I'm so very impressed with this progress." Oh but it made me glow inside. "You have made such strides since your earlier unwilling-ness to embrace your new profession."

"I've found a home in it."

"At last," he added.

"Yes, at last. As you've found a welcome home within your profession, my Doctor-General."

"I don't follow."

"With the cadavers, I mean, the carving out of your niche within the cadavers."

"Yes, yes."

"The new direction, so reviled initially. I marvel at the response you've gotten since commencing work in the morgue." My place in his life as pupil and confidante had grown with the passing weeks. A loose informality had descended, leaving us, sometimes, sharing the evening meal or strolling out into the night together. As often as not, we'd pass the hours chatting over liqueur in the outer chamber, zipping off, say, to the morgue to fetch a clutch of severed heads, piling them carefully on the back-seat of his limousine before rushing back to the Ministry to inspect them. Through it all, the inner chamber remained sacred, cloaked in a seriousness and purpose that instantly dispelled the frivolity and ease of our relationship outside. I was glad for that.

Equally, my relationship with Hakan had moved forward. I long to recount each tiny detail of our turnings toward each other, but fear it would stretch into an eternity (though not an unhappy one). Suffice it to say that he returned as he'd said he would, coming wet and exhausted from out of the night to my door and staying, two or three times each week. We'd hang his clothes to dry and curl up by the heater, talking until the dim winter light came to the eastern sky and we'd sleep. I told him each detail of our Prime Minister's progress and what he'd said, never omitting any detail or feeling it as a betrayal of that courageous man. Hakan loved him as I did, now that he knew of his fragile condition. (So I believed.) He'd tell me more each time of his own life, reassuring me he was fed and decently sheltered from the cold. Indeed, he looked healthy, slim and muscular, always vigorous and warm when he lay near me. We slept naked and entangled as puppies, curled together in the blankets which, that long-ago first night, had been his nest alone.

He told me his politics, invoking Lucrezia as one might a symbol or a god, betraying the clumsiness of his understanding of her, her complexities and grief. But I didn't scold him, letting his ignorance lie, divinely wed to his youthful hunger.

"And this is the leader we seek," he confessed to me under the mysterious howling of another winter storm backed up against the hills. He held a small picture, clipped from a newspaper, which he'd drawn from out of his bandanna. I looked for a moment and handed it back to him. "No, keep it," he instructed. "I've brought it for you. I want you to understand, you see, and maybe find out from the Prime Minister something about this man."

"Who is he?" I asked, wondering about the vaguely familiar face.

"He was the leader of the last opposition."

"Oh yes, I remember him. He fell from a balloon. He's dead, isn't he?"

"We think he might still be alive."

"After a fall like that?"

"It might not have been him who fell. No one is very sure."

"And if it wasn't? If he is still alive?"

"He could lead us. There are men, and ties within the government. If he were to rally the people it would only be a matter of days." His politics thrilled me, if only for the fire it put in his heavenly eyes. To see them charged, suddenly, with passion was breathtaking. I fed the flames.

"No doubt you *would* come to power if he were alive."

"*We* would come to power," he corrected me. "And he *is* still alive, I can be sure of it. You must ask him questions now."

"The Prime Minister?"

"Yes. You've gained his confidence, and now you must use it."

"I really couldn't. He's an old man."

"One who trusts you."

"And for good reason. I only agreed to tell you what he said, not to interrogate him or go digging around for anything." This is the point at which, a little drunk, he kissed me. I felt his slim, muscular chest brushing against mine, and when he pressed closer, his heart beat so strongly I could feel it pushing on my sternum. Of course I said I'd try.

"Down, Mr. uh, uh, down I say," the coach shouted. Things weren't going terribly well. My erotic sensitivities had risen. Stroked and strummed as I was so often now by my rebel friend, I found the inextinguishable flame flared with emplacement of the bag, or "device." It had gone far beyond the coach's dousing powers.

"Perhaps if you repeat the part about his boils, the maggots in his boils," I suggested, wanting to be as helpful as I could. Nothing seemed to work. Hakan's lovely body swam so convincingly through my mind that nothing the coach could say would calm me. I blamed Flessinger and Ponz, really, who had forever wed the image of him, Hakan, with the sack which contained me. I couldn't possibly explain this to the coach, for it would involve confessing my love and its consummation. So, each week I clamped the bag gamely on and hoped for the best. Once snugly fit, however, the needles inevitably began their brief dance, peaking quickly and remaining there for as long as it took me to come. The coach wasn't at all pleased, and had even ceased his ritual pep talk and prayer (which had, the first few weeks, marked the conclusion of each session).

I knew it meant trouble. Word would eventually reach my Doctor-General, undermining his sense of my general progress, and changes would be ordered. I wouldn't miss the coach and his stuffy little bower, but I feared the prospect of what my Doctor-General might have waiting in the wings. Things could go from bad to worse, I knew, as easily as they could get better.

On this, it turned out, my last afternoon with the coach, I was left alone to clean the bag. He was drained by the futile task he'd set for himself, and stumbled out of the cozy den without even a word of farewell. It made me sad to have disappointed him by my failure, and I bent to my task under a cloud of melancholy.

Seabirds could be heard calling outside the small oval windows. Their shadows cut across me as they lifted off from their perches and sank briefly into the sky. I saw them recover, heavy wings opened wide, pulling them back onto a steady course up and out toward the water.

I opened the window, turning it on its two metal pins, and leaned my head out into the late winter air. The sun was lost in a haze of wood smoke and mist, tracing a course across the low horizon. It would soon sink and die, leaving the city for another long night. The Prime Minister would be at the Salon within the hour. I had moved his appointments to the evening so he could come under cover of darkness, exposing his raw face to the open air without fear of detection. Really, he had nothing to fear. He looked nothing like himself yet.

In the quiet before the Prime Minister's arrival, behind my mask in the dark chamber, I sometimes felt as my Doctor-General must feel before *our* daily therapies . . . alone, supine upon the couch, enbagged. Small anticipations and plans crossed my mind, the prospect of some fresh development, firm muscle where the previous week was flaccid flesh. I'd review the simple words or gestures, some subtle manipulation of the face, say, that might lift decades of agony from the Prime Minister's lips. The patient's eyes would sparkle then with the clear recognition of my virtues as an artisan (and/or human being).

The door slipped open and he came in, dropping his coat by the rack. I perched on my stool, letting the little rollers run back and forth, traversing over and over a slight, silent measure of the hard linoleum floor. It was utterly dark, but he didn't bump me, having by now memorized the short passage from the door to his chair.

"I'm ready, Doctor." He settled quickly, with no preliminary chitchat. "You may turn on the lights." I pressed the two buttons in the wall. The power engaged behind them, and the brilliant chrome fixtures disappeared into the light.

"Keep your eyes closed, sir, for a moment, while they adjust." He was my child, the cherished object of my labors. "Don't let the

light make you squint too tightly. It might wrinkle your new skin."
He let his face fall slack, loosening along the cheek and jowl.
With each small letting go the surface sank against the bone. He
was pure flesh now, a bit thin and hollow around the eyes, but
freed from the wreckage of the earlier constructions. There were
some scars, little slipups by his previous doctor (and two or three
of my own). But they didn't concern me. It would all disappear
again soon enough.

"I feel positively naked," he whispered, turning to look at me.
"The air blowing across my skin. It's all very embarrassing." He
smiled as he spoke, revealing some pleasure in his predicament. I
watched the skin stretch during our exchange, trying to gain a
measure of its health. It was pale, the color of thin milk, and supple, lying comfortably slack and transparent over the face of his
skull. His eyes were particularly deep. They lay low inside the
obiculeris oculi. The skin draped cleanly over the ridges and
stretched along toward his cheek like a snowfield. I ran my fingers
around the rims, letting them slide down either side of the nose,
pressing occasionally to test his response. He kept still like a good
patient.

"Do you feel any pain, anything at all?" I reached my open
hand over the width of his face, kneading it like a lump of dough,
testing the pliability of his features. He mumbled from within my
grip.

"No pain. Just a, a tingling."

"A tingling?" I wiped the spittle from my palm.

"All over my face, like it had fallen asleep, the way an arm
does?" I pulled at his nostrils to gauge their stretch, noting this
interesting symptom. Perhaps it *had* been asleep. No one else had
ever spent so prolonged a period within a mask. I had no idea
what was normal.

"Is it hard to move?" I pulled his brow away from the skull.

"Not at all. Feels quite light and mobile, actually."

Who would have thought this was the same monster who'd come to me only a few short weeks before? His face was an unnerving combination of freshness and age; the milky, soft texture hung in ancient folds over bone. Exercise, exposure, and some therapeutic oils were needed to bring it back to life. It would take four weeks, at minimum. We began that day with a eucalyptus-citronella rub to brace the flaccid skin. I plugged his nose with cotton and lathered the light oil vigorously.

"Have you a companion, Mr. Sludge, an animal or friend?" He put it so delicately. I couldn't tell him honestly about Hakan, though I could easily devise a convenient fiction to stand for the truth.

"I have a dog, sir. A very smart and friendly young dog."

"How nice for you. Is he a big dog?" Oh, his interest made my heart swell.

"Yes, quite big, sir, and very healthy. A strong young dog, and brave too." I pulled the towel from his face, watching the splotchy redness I had raised fade away. "His name is Hakan." What daring. It made my pulse race to say it.

"What a lovely name, Hakan. Very unusual, too."

"Yes, sir. I believe it's Turkish, or perhaps Norwegian. One can never be sure." I pulled a large white towel from the steamer and covered his head with it. "He was a stray. I found him the night of the first snow, just this winter."

"Very humane of you." He mumbled through the warm, wet towel. "There's many a citizen who'd have just turned such a dog away into the cold."

"Or turned him in to the authorities," I added.

"Which is actually more humane, one must believe, than

leaving him to forage in the wild." The Animal Control was well known for the painlessness of its procedures (though I'd never considered them kind).

"I'm just glad I found him; he has changed my life. Love is a strange and wonderful thing."

"Yes it is. A very demanding taskmaster, too." I replaced the towel with a fresh one.

"How do you mean, sir?"

"Oh, just a thought. Only a leader knows, I would imagine." He paused. I waited quietly and occupied myself with my work. The towel took the heated aloe nicely.

"Love compels the leader, Mr. Sludge, just as it compels each of us in our more mundane relationships." I let his eyes free, nodding in agreement. then I squeezed a thick layer of grease over the ocular ridges. "The leader loves his people, passionately. His longing for them is profound, consuming, Mr. Sludge. It's not a comforting or comfortable thing. It's a terrible, overarching love that emanates from him."

"I've felt it, sir, I have." He could not know how true it was, having no knowledge of the laboratory of Flessinger and Ponz, the wires and the chair.

"I'm glad, and I'm sorry for you. If you've been touched by the force of this love, I'm truly sorry."

"No need, I know that love to be true. Terrible and overarching, just as you've said, but a true and pure love. I've felt it quite directly."

"I dare not ask, and I hope you'll forgive me for that. I protect myself, sometimes, from knowledge. You do understand?" I let my silence stand as an answer, laying a third towel down over the grease and pressing on it with both hands. His mouth remained free, and he used it. "I've crushed whole generations, so utter and complete was my love for them. Health is a curious thing." I coated my fingers with okra and passed them along his lips as he spoke. "A leader has certain needs, an unusual depth of hunger. It's so much harder to love a multitude, a city, than to love another man. I can never be sure I'm doing enough."

"Could you feel their love?" I asked in the silence. "Was it ever clear enough that you could feel it?"

"Sometimes, yes, if I'd meet one, in the prison say, or one of the men in the hospitals. They're more expressive when they're dying. I don't know why. It's hard if someone's happy, I guess. They get stupid about love. They don't see it clearly, mistaking it for ease or comfort. A leader does not provide ease or comfort."

"No," I agreed, increasing the pressure on his mouth. "The men in the prisons know that, and the men in the hospitals."

"That's right, yes. They've felt my love more directly, I've really shown it to them, quite severely. No pussyfooting or coddling like we're tempted to do with the children. When you're sick or incarcerated a lot of illusions get swept away. I'd like to arrest everyone, at some point, just to clarify the nature of our relationship."

"But what stops you?" I asked, for the first time given a glimpse of the human dimension of politics. "What prevents you from realizing the fullest expression of your love?"

"Fear, Mr. Sludge. Fear and the law. A leader is elected for his awful capacity to love, yet the people instinctively fear his expression of it. I draw close, tantalizing them with my image, yet they always become frightened and run, unwilling to endure my true embrace. They love to hear the cracking of the whip, the drums and boots, but only from a distance."

"Yet they ask you for your love, they demand it of you."

"And I give it, unceasingly. I love them as myself."

"Yes, exactly."

"But it's all pretense for them, adolescent flirting. Few have the courage to enter into our Criminal and Health systems, where my love is least encumbered by law."

"I know it," I affirmed, feeling his frustration with all my heart. What a damnable paradox our leader suffered, elected and celebrated for the capacity of which we then denied him the expression. Set up as a burning flame, a torch in whose light we yearned to bask, and then condemned to burn out alone, fed no fuel, given no tinder to touch, the people too frightened by the warm flame they themselves desired to come even close enough to feel it.

"We pay lip service to love, but when it comes into our lives and shackles us, we cry foul. People think they can just change their minds and run away. It's maddening. At least the prisons and hospitals can demand fidelity, of a sort . . . "

"The people can be so selfish," I consoled.

"Yes, they can. And yet, for all their selfish stupidity, they have glimpsed something, some of the grace and, can I say it, transcendence of my love as I wish to express it. They still flock to the pageants and thrill to my rhetoric. Oh, it's incantatory, all those fine, rough, marching words. I'll just beat and lash them with my tongue, and still they cheer. You've got to admire them for it. If only they'd make up their minds, take the next bold step."

"Humble themselves."

"As they should. It's not me so much as my position that demands it. Someone will come after I've gone. There will always be a leader."

I found that there were tears dripping off my face into his towel. I let them soak among the oils and lotions that would heal him. Blessed and condemned to be our leader, he was our Prime Minister. When I turned away late that evening, letting him back out into the night, it was all I could do to withhold my embrace.

*   *   *

No stars pierced the sky, nor lights reflected back off the overcast. A fire burned high on the bare hillside. Its orange flame danced weakly in the frozen air, offering the occasional blackened silhouette of branches and a tiny, fluttering tricolor being carried around the flames. Was Hakan up there, I wondered, with them? Would her song be sung, again, wobbling richly through the winter air to touch my ears, and why? What standard did she bear for them, what spirit? Was the night their enemy or friend? I watched the Prime Minister wander away into that same night and could not help but love him whose demise they sought; I felt, for the first time, that they loved him too. They could not say it, and perhaps did not even recognize the embrace contained within their hatred. I wondered how much he knew of their plot against him, and whether it was an end he in some ways desired. And what did he know of me?

(Winter is burdened with the image of frightened, half-starved soldiers crawling through snow on their bellies, our army sneaking into the occupied city by night and taking it so swiftly the enemy had no time to fire even a shot. I could hear them now, in the silence, as I stood in the snow. What a glorious morning it must have been. The city was liberated and the supply lines thrown open to allow food, finally, in. Who knows what it was really like, or even what of it was true? We know nothing of war in our time, only nostalgia. Old people bore us with the pain of their memory. We shut our ears to them; they are erased, and style is the past's last trace. Children dress as soldiers now, snug in their camouflage fatigues, sporting bandannas and belts made to carry ammunition. Do they wish for guns, or an enemy, or war? I can only walk past them, uncertain as to what the fashion, ultimately, refers, to what desire it finally represents.)

*   *   *

I woke to the sound of the bath. Steam billowed fiercely against the tiles. Hakan lay under the faucet, letting the water tumble over his feet. Its level rose along his ribs, the little shoreline crawling like a loving tide past his sternum and up his slim brown chest. How I envied the water, that it could so surround and comfort him. He lay immersed, his eyes closed dreamily, and let his ears submerge into the silent rumbling. If I yelled or beat against the metal tub he might hear me. As it was, I could stand and watch him, touching the whole and glorious length of his body with my eyes. Were he to see me it would change the pleasure, bringing an easy smile of pride to his devilish, angelic face. I was glad for his brief innocence.

The sound of the church bells reached down into our street, a dull, distant ringing muffled in the snow. They rang eleven or twelve, I wasn't certain. I put fresh water on to boil, pulled my soft flannel nightshirt on, and cleared the tangled blankets from where we'd lain. There would be no appointments today. Tomorrow I was due to visit my Doctor-General. Then there would be the matter of the coach to discuss, and something more.

"Come scrub me," I heard him call, his breaking voice lilting through each strangely inflected word. "I want to be made very clean." He'd dunked himself completely under and now sat straight up. His dark hair dripped wet against his head. I kneeled by the tub and took him by the shoulders, scrubbing with the bath brush. Soaping him along his ribs and spine, I let my hand pause for a while on his beating heart. He smiled and splashed, shivering with the pressure of the tiny bristles. The impatient kettle beckoned, and I rushed to take it from the stove. The tea things were arranged. I poured the pot full and returned to the tub with my offering. Hakan stood wrapped in my terrycloth robe.

Where lay my Doctor-General in the divine hour we then

passed, chaste and loving, sharing our special feeling through silence, words, the brush of hand across hand? What position did he, whose wisdom and support I sought as guide to my life, take regarding our love so expressed? I had such trouble, still, with the distinctions. In that hour, my hand never strayed near the target areas (as so long ago outlined by my advisor and confidante) yet I believe I touched him more deeply and profoundly than ever my frequent acts of molestation could. Where was his soul in the eyes of the law? Was my mingling there an act of penetration? Surely it must be so. Simple insertion of the penis was nothing compared to the depth of my entry into him in that hour of conversation and glances. And if allowed, even applauded by the law, would our depth of fellow feeling ever mitigate the imputation of violence carried inside the word "molestation"? Was it molestation if I loved him and he loved me? And what of my Doctor-General's repeated penetrations into my soul? Could I really, within the context of my conviction, be termed a freely consenting adult?

These black meanderings did not descend to interrupt our moment together. Only in the dim minutes after he left did they rise up inside me, together with a wave of anger and frustration. For all the progress I'd made with the Doctor-General (coming to a level of friendship and sharing unusual between two men) I'd not come even a small step closer to comprehension of the legal distinctions between love and molestation. Apparently there were none.

Hakan, clean and freshly scrubbed, warm within my baggy dungarees and fisherman's sweater, trundled up the street toward the university and, eventually, the hills. I was his lover. It was I, what I was best at, and most fully expressed through—the loving of him. He sensed that and loved me for it in return.

* * *

The morning had gone, though the dim light remained unchanged. The sun might have been anywhere. I was anxious to get up, to drop in on the lobster man and invite him out for lunch or coffee. His return home in the dark night left me more eager to speak with him than was perhaps reasonable. I felt as though there was a question to which he alone had the answer. Something about the beginnings of this perplexing turn in my new-new life, the why or wherefore of my descent into—was it politics? His position at the center of this enormous wheel seemed to imply he had access to answers, answers to my most basic questions.

I tucked away the blankets and dressed. Soup was left to simmer while I was away. The hallway was empty and smelled of cat urine as it almost always did. The lobster man's door was open, so I knocked briskly and stepped in, ready to give him my friendly greetings. But the room was empty, utterly. Useless wire hung from bent hooks where the pugilists had been. Dim faded rectangles framed the broken hardware. A few empty sheets of paper still littered the dirty carpet, blank or largely so. The high piles of manuscript pages had been removed, taken away with the pugilists and pots and pans. My heart jumped at the sound of someone moving in the kitchen, pushing a knife, I thought, back and forth across metal.

I called out hello and heard nothing, no voice or cessation in the scraping. The doorway was only a few feet from me and I stepped toward it. There was an old woman inside, her large, squat back toward me, scraping wax off the metal edge of the counter.

"Hello," I repeated. "Do you know where the fellow who lives here has gone?" She didn't move except to continue scraping. Small trails of wax twisted off the dull chrome with each pass of the knife. "Hello," I said loudly. She stopped abruptly and turned around, brandishing the knife, then braced herself against the counter.

"I'm a friend of the man who lived here." I was almost shouting. She gestured to me to shut up and pulled paper and pen from her ample frock.

"Go away," she wrote in simple block letters. I took the pen from her.

"I'm a friend of the man who lived here," I wrote, my hand tiring as early as the fifth word. She rolled her eyes.

"You have the rent?"

"No," I wrote, pausing to formulate a brief question. She took the pen from me.

"He left no address, no rent. Go away."

"When?" I wrote. I looked at her, hoping she'd read sympathy in my face.

"Good-bye," she wrote, and pushed me out the door, slamming it shut behind me.

The empty wires hung in my memory. Did the lobster man have the strength to pull them so roughly from their hardware, even if he'd wanted to? Traces of wood could be seen still clinging to the teeth of the screws. It wasn't at all like him. I went to the foyer and tried my thin key on his mailbox. It turned and opened easily. Inside were a clutch of letters. I took them, envying him their bulk and number, and returned to my room.

The first was a solicitation disguised as personal correspondence. It appeared to be handwritten, both inside and out, but a slipup in alignment showed it was made by a machine. What treachery. It was from a provincial university, evidently the lobster man's alma mater, and was an appeal for funds. The machine carried on the conceit that it was an old classmate who'd seen my friend's name in the phone book, sparking fond memories, blah,

blah, blah, of good old Berlin or some such name. I threw it in the trash.

A second envelope bore his name in typescript. There was no stamp and no return address. Evidently a messenger had brought it. Inside there was a ballot of some sort, a yellow slip of paper with a series of options neatly typed. They were as follows: Cyproterone Acetate; Prolixin; Benperidol; Medroxyprogesterone (depot); Stilbestrol; All of the Above; Surgery. There was nothing more in the envelope.

The largest piece was a long envelope that had been stuffed quite full. Its edges had frayed from handling, and it was wrinkled, having evidently been dropped in the snow. The address was scrawled in a messy familiar hand, the stamp affixed upside down, and no return address was given. It was, in fact, the lobster man's own handwriting, I realized, slitting the edge open with a knife. Twenty or thirty typed pages were enclosed. I opened them up and read. "What was the precise nature of your desire?" etc., etc. It was some sort of story, set in our city. A small slip of paper fell out, a dim, faded scrap of mimeo bearing three words: "No, thank you." That was all. What on earth did he mean by sending this short story to himself? I put it with the mysterious ballot. Only two letters left.

The penultimate missive came in a plain envelope with a neatly typed address. The stamp was colorful and foreign, and the return address appeared (in the continental manner) type-written, on the reverse side. "de Heer Scheeperleider" it said simply, with no street or number given. I opened the thin envelope, letting the sharp knife slip along its edge, and shook the one-page letter free. It was dated nearly six weeks ago. The text was completely foreign. "Beste Beeste" it began. "Leven heir verrukkelijk is," and on and on. What language was this? I scanned the crowded page and, to my horror, recognized a few recurring words: "Lucrezia," "Mr. Sludge," and "Sludgje." "Met je in oranje, zwart, en groen," "Scheepje," it closed. I placed this alone on the table.

The last was the smallest, a heavy stock envelope in soft pastel blue, the lobster man's name elegantly scripted, and "Mimi" written in flowing hand at the upper left. A soft, flowery perfume wafted from it as I split the flap from its glue spot. It was a solicitation for a corporate laundering service. I dropped it in the trash with the university's cloying plea for money.

Outside, a flash of lightning broke from the clouds. I waited for the sound of rain, used only to spring and summer storms, and then looked to see snow swirling up and down, beating silently at the window. Thunder rumbled in. It was the letter from de Heer Scheeperleider that interested me most, and gave me the fewest clues. Surely the municipal library would have the books I needed to identify the language and to translate it. There was no one to whom I could entrust this menacing note.

I passed the day by my window looking for Hakan. What shelter was there in the hills? Had he even reached it? I hoped, and believed, that he'd never left the city, the storm settling too quickly for him or anyone else to go. He was somewhere, in a student garret, a warm café, maybe even bunking up in the municipal shelter. Even if he had not made it out, the streets were quickly becoming impassable. Safety demanded he stay put, where he was, however near that might be. Still, I stared hard into the storm, hoping, hungry for a glimpse of him.

At some point in the lost afternoon, perhaps it was dusk, I drifted into sleep at my station, resting my head on a pillow against the glass. In my scattered perceptions I kept seeing the lobster man walking toward me in the storm, his progress and mood undisturbed by its violence. His eyes penetrated the dim, murky light with power and ease, engaging mine from nearly a hundred yards distance. He walked toward me, nothing more, over and over, the storm raging but forgotten in my fixation on his eyes. He never reached me. Thunder rumbled through my dream, distant and near, and the storm's fury struck down all around us. It rose to an unbearable peak, the sharp electrical air cracking open beside me, and I awoke to someone knocking impatiently at the door.

It was Hakan.

He was covered in a mantle of snow and ice, his face bright red and wet from sweat and the melting frost. He smiled and shivered, standing in the doorway dumb and immobile. I took him by the shoulders and guided him to the tub room. "You miserable boy," I scolded, "out in a storm like this without so much as a proper hat." I rubbed his frozen hair vigorously with a towel, feeling it melt and become pliable under the slightest touch.

"Is not so bad," he slurred, his mouth still spastic with shivers. "Very spectacular, the lightning." His eyes lit up with the report, his accent made thicker by the cold. I turned the hot water on, letting the room fill with steam.

"Undress," I instructed. "And don't get in the tub yet, the steam should be enough for now." I closed the door and went to stir the soup, glad for my prescience. What a relief it was to have him there, shivering in the heat. To doctor him was my greatest desire. I set a big fire in the hearth (inadvertently tossing the lobster man's story in with the burning trash) and readied our dinner.

He ate the food eagerly, hardly stopping to say a word. The bowl was empty, wiped clean with a thick end of bread, before he even looked up from it. I gave him a second bowl, which he approached with some calm and contentment. "My neighbor left," I told him, wondering how much he knew already. "Very suddenly, last night while we were sleeping." He chewed a hunk of buttered bread, washing it down with milk.

"That's too bad. Were you friends?"

"Well, yes. I knew him. Don't you remember?"

"Remember what?"

"He arranged my job at the Salon." Hakan made a moustache, drinking his milk in big mouthfuls.

"Oh, yes. But your neighbor was not my contact. He may be with us, but I am not working through him. There are others." The fire spat and settled, letting a shower of orange sparks fly upward.

"Who is your contact there?"

He leaned over and kissed me lightly on the cheek. "You," he said, just like that. He could be so evasive.

"Yes, of course. But who was it before me?"

"Doctor Cotton. It must be the head man, you see, to have you with the Prime Minister. Now what is it about your neighbor? Where did he go?" I looked in his eyes. The dancing fire reflected there. His irises opened, big and black as the night outside. How did it feel to live behind those eyes, bombarded by the sweeping tide of everyone looking in, drawn in by those astonishing, open portals? It was as though he had no guard at the gate, no border. A man without skin might be better protected against the world than he. He left his mouth slightly open, his wet tongue at play among the teeth. The flesh of his face was healthy and soft, graced with thick, silken eyebrows that knit neatly together above his wide nose and arched away above his eyes.

"I don't know," I said in answer to his question. "It was all very sudden and mysterious."

"No one else that knows him?"

"No one I know. Except, I thought, you." I went to the small table by the window and picked up the two letters, handing them to Hakan. "I got these from his mailbox today."

He sniffed them, passing them along his delicate fingertips

before pulling the letters from their envelopes. The ballot didn't seem to interest him. "Have you heard of this Scheeperleider before?"

"No, never. Have you?"

"Just rumors," he said enigmatically. "Nothing I can be sure of. It's a Dutch name."

"And the text, is it in Dutch also?" He opened the letter and scanned it, sniffing again as though he'd been trained to.

"Yes, I think so. I'm quite sure it is."

"Do you know anyone who speaks it?"

"No, I didn't know anyone spoke it anymore. I thought they all spoke English now."

"Yes, possibly," I agreed. "I think we can find a dictionary at the library. But what are the rumors, the ones about Scheeperleider?"

Hakan slipped the letter back into its envelope, inspecting the stamp and the date of its postmark. He set it on the floor, by the ballot, and sat thinking. "Scheeperleider is maybe from the city, you see. Some among the rebels think he is the opposition leader, the old one who was supposed to die."

"The man you've been looking for."

"Yes, but we've not managed to make contact with him. He's apparently a strange, crazy man."

"But the letter."

"The letter could be nothing. He wrote thousands of them. He's still writing them. I'm surprised you haven't gotten one. That's how he came to our attention."

"He wrote to you?"

"To everyone. No one knows how he got all the addresses. He's been writing for several years now. Sometimes he claims to be the Prime Minister, sometimes the old opposition leader. He only writes to the rebels, so far as we can tell. Though I've never seen one in Dutch before. He seems to know an awful lot, things no one else could have known, incidents."

"But you've never made contact?"

"No one can find him. He leaves no return address, as you can see. The letters come always from different cities, Groningen, Baarn, Rotterdam. We haven't been able to track him down."

"He might just be some old crank writing letters?"

"No, he's someone all right. He knows too much to be just anyone. The question is whether he's the man we need, our leader."

Hakan became feverish in the night. I made him stay in bed the next day to rest while I went out on my errands and my trip to the library. It shouldn't be too hard, I thought, with a proper dictionary and a few spare hours. The letter itself was only one page, and that in a script so florid and chaotic it probably amounted to no more than a hundred words. I hadn't been to the library in weeks.

The great façade of the building dwarfed the public square that was its terrace. Anyone brave enough to sit out in the cold could enjoy hot drinks and pastry at a café there, with its scattered metal tables. The waitress, in brown fur-about and muffler, scooted around the square this bright morning brandishing a broom and sweeping deep snowdrifts from the tables. Small plastic cushions were provided so that one might sit in relative comfort.

I passed up the treat, wanting no delay, and scaled the wide stone steps. At either end of the broad stairway two muscular stone serpents curled demonically around scepters. Mounted high upon the scepters (tickled by the impressive reach of the serpents' unraveled tongues) were a pair of apples, smoothly polished marble, each with a delicate crown of stem and leaves.

I found an empty desk in a far dusty corner of the Reference Room and opened my letter under the lamp. "Beste Beeste," it began (as I have earlier reported). "My dear animal, beast, brute." How curious. I chose "brute." "Life here delightful is." Telling. What an odd construction. "I and my recollections with tears and laughter here stand." They'd known each other before, perhaps? In what sense "stand"? I marked this passage with a red check-mark to indicate my uncertainty. "Are you still the same old chicken fucker?" I blushed and marked this section as well. I hadn't known that about the lobster man. "I am. She has new place soon, thank God. Changing is in the clouds standing, glorious colors. I for its through-going anxious am. Soon. Oh God woman Lucrezia, with her divinity standing." Was the image metaphorical? "Your Mr. Sludge is also by Lucrezia standing? Can he you into me make, so no travels to do? Can he a new Lucrezia make?" At this point the extended punctuation interrupted. A line of tall exclamation marks and curled question marks extended across the page several times over. "In a ship (my name!) we soon to you return come. A ship! All times an ant fucker! I hold of you all times, with your details, love of my life. My garment dress and mask me well fit. I am again him, or me. The opposite. Little Sludge would very proud be. You delicious ant fucker. When the before year begins, in the melting time, springs the plan. With you in orange, black, and green (small) vessel." Thus ended the communiqué. A very beautiful language, Dutch, I reflected. Poetic even in its translation.

I guessed he would be traveling soon. Perhaps this was the vacation at which the lobster man had so recently joined him . . . one couldn't be certain. But then it did mention "the melting time" (a very popular time among tourists wanting to visit our city). Perhaps he meant to take his holiday in spring, "the plan" being the itinerary he'd set with my old friend. I folded the small page neatly and tucked it in my breast pocket. It was well past noon and I feared Hakan would soon be growing restive.

Traversing the busy square, toward the lane leading home, I spotted my Doctor-General scribbling ferociously at a sunny café table. His greatcoat was drawn up around him, and he'd managed somehow to have a wide slab of wood secured for his tabletop. It was against this that he pressed his pen down mightily. The long, unwinding scrawl had already filled several pages.

"Doctor-General," I called politely, tipping my head to him. "What a surprise." He looked up from his work, quite startled and upset. The carefully balanced wood block spilled to the ground, releasing the pages. I stooped politely to gather them up.

"Ah, my friend. I hadn't expected . . . you." He slowly recovered his usual tact and calm. "What a pleasure." There was a second seat and he allowed me to sit with him. I brushed the dirty snow from off his pages, arresting the incipient runs of ink with delicate blottings of my shirtsleeve.

"Your pages." I smiled warmly.

"Thank you. You'll forgive my dizziness. I'm nearly finished composing my paper on the early surgeries." He brandished the soggy notes as evidence. "Yesterday's storm was quite a blessing. I've not had such a block of free time in weeks."

He glanced down at his shoes. "About our meeting this evening." His wheedling tone worried me. Was he going to cancel on me? "Could you possibly come a bit early and help me out? I have a few final details for the paper; I don't think I can manage them alone."

"Oh, could I?" I asked back coolly, masking my pleasure.

"If you would, yes. Half-past seven or so."

"Consider it done." Possibly I'd be tidying up his prose, correcting a logical error or two. Obviously he couldn't send the thing out untested.

And so our brief visit passed, with gaiety and pleasant chatter. It allowed me to glimpse what I had been told lay at the end of my long road back to mental health—the erection of normal friendships with attractive, powerful men (that is to say, adult heterosexuality). Could we be buddies, cuffing each other severely, and bouncing ribald bon mots back and forth like tennis balls? It seemed, for a moment, that such a thing was possible.

At home, Hakan lay in bed, a volume of Cervantes propped in his cosseted lap. I summoned him to the table. "I've done it," I announced, brandishing the translation. "Though it doesn't seem to be much more than travel plans." We laid the little missive down, brushing away a mess of bread crumbs and cheese left by my hungry boarder.

"'Changing is in the clouds standing'?" he read aloud. "Are you sure of the correct translation?"

Impudent child. "Of course I am. I took great care with this. Every word, just as the dictionary said."

"I think it is more than travel. 'Changing,' you see. And this 'garment dress and mask. I am again him, or me. The opposite.' What could he mean?"

"You said he was a bit off, didn't you?"

"Well, yes, some think so." He held the paper up close to his face as if its meaning were a force, like gravity, diminished exponentially by distance. "But I think there's something here. 'I am again him.' He wouldn't need a mask just to travel, would he, if he was not somebody?"

"Perhaps he's sensitive to the sun?" I guessed, not wanting to get too upset about my neighbor's sudden rush to his holiday.

"But 'I am again him'? The man's in disguise. Who could he mean by 'him'?" We held the scrap up to the light, Hakan sniffing again at the original. I'd not overlooked any text, and I was certain the translation was, largely, correct. "I've got to show this to my comrades," Hakan announced at last (and somewhat melodramatically). The suggestion would not have troubled me were he able to simply invite them over for tea, discussing the letter and its meaning by a warm fire, say, before going to the Eichelberger for an evening snack. But he couldn't. He'd be going to the hills again, taking my heart with him.

I took this occasion as a chance to clean and rearrange our little nest so it in no way resembled the apartment I'd moved into five months before. Five months. It seemed so much more distant than that. So much had intervened, I could easily have spent a lifetime traversing the great path I'd traveled in this my new, or new-new life. And yet it also seemed like yesterday that I had stepped off the train and into the waiting gaze of my Doctor-General. If these short months had spanned a lifetime, they had also merely occupied a moment, the entirety both infinite in its extension and confined within a dimensionless point.

Was this a feature of my mental illness? The Doctor-General had never mentioned it, or I had never mentioned it to him. It was tied, somehow, to my balloon fantasies, etc., my occasional dispersal into space, all location dissolved within a ubiquity of presence (as realized through the medium of "the view," it extending so completely and pristinely). Really, there was no one with whom I'd yet breached the topic. The lobster man had been as likely a candidate as any, but alas. My Doctor-General could not afford the anxiety such a complex admission would bring. Perhaps Hakan would be interested. I thought it best to wait and see.

Oh, I missed the boy already, but I found I was enjoying it. I felt, oddly, relieved by this hiatus in our infant love. Rather than burdening me with grief, his disappearance out the door had drawn a weight away, lifting a mantle of sweet sensation off my body. My air became uncluttered and clean, my mind spacious.

I anticipated his return from the hills as a point of new beginning, intending then to ask him to stay. I had so many books to
read. I'd never get to them, but *he* would. If he stayed. I'd set a
course of study. He could read and instruct me. I would show him
the collections, arrange travels, tutor him in all his basic skills . . .

I pulled the drapes down and bundled them up with the rest
of the garbage. If we lived together, it would be without drapes. A
few minutes was all it took to strip the decorations from the wall
and stack them neatly in a pile. Large, garish prints weren't welcome, though some of my smaller treasures might yet be
remounted. I had little furniture to fuss over. I brewed some tea
and sat down among the clutter. The table and chairs weren't
needed. (How nice to have a low, elegant surface and sit around it
on cushions, as the Japanese were said to do.) If my bulky dining
set were removed, the room might really open up. Would Hakan
attend the university? Oh, it was so hard to say (and even harder
to refrain from asking).

It was nearly five and well into the gloaming. The eastern sky
had turned black, and the west become a pool of iron at the edge
of the sea. The news kiosk had fresh copies of the evening edition.
My table at the Eichelberger was free and the hostess charming
(as always), plying me with hot toddies and a selection of day-old
pastries. Why did I ever leave? I had an appointment with the
Doctor-General, a prospect I quite looked forward to. The newspaper lay unopened, acting as a coaster for the delightful bever-
ages. I simply stared out the window, glimpsing myself, occasionally, in reflection. The café filled and emptied twice in the two
hours I sat dreaming. The bell tolling once after seven said it was
time to catch a tram to the darkened palace of the Ministry of
Health (and the evening voice of my inquisitor). My Doctor-General's lights would be the only ones burning at this hour.

* * *

Wasn't there once the belief that crystalline spheres, in ever wider concentricities, held each part of our blackened sky, filling the void we now perceive with infinitely thin sheets of glass? The planets each rode in their own glass ball, the stars sharing the outermost shell. We were at the center, nesting inside it all, unmoved and unmoving, set here to watch the infinite variety of the crystalline spinning. *Lamina, lamella, pellicle.* No bird or fallen rock could move among them without shattering the sky. Birds flew through ether. Nothing outside it moved, except in concert with the tuneful turning of the spheres. Their fit and slip and slide produced a sound so pure and heavenly, its harmony filled us up; it occupied our minds and souls so completely that the sound could not be heard. Both interior and exterior, we could not "take it in."

Was it a winter sky? I've not seen the bare rock islands that gave us this world, nor the sky that hung above them, but I can imagine it in this late winter night. A quality of air returns me there, some obscure purity in what I breathe or see. Perhaps that is what carries the thought, now as then. Aristotle's last breath is said still to be mingling, tickling our tongues with every mouthful of air we draw into our lungs. Does it touch me inside, triggering the invisible shives? The idea is mine as much as the breath is his.

The tram might have shattered each stratum in turn had it run the course of comets. But the worn iron rails kept the small car on its track toward the Ministry, saving the mythical spheres from the embarrassment of breaking. What drew my thoughts away if not the breath of Aristotle? Admittedly that theory had holes. Why not the thoughts of Aquinas, for example, if the track of my mind lay in the particular turns of the air I breathed? Why not my Doctor-General, whose breath I would soon share so intimately, locked in our airless room? Did I kiss my rebel boyfriend so intractably in order that I might enter his mind? That could be.

Why not, then, a therapeutic kiss from the Doctor-General? Our mouths locked together so that I might come to see the world precisely as he did. Weren't we engaged in that same pursuit, but at a distance, him pouring his mind into mine from so far away that the transfer took months instead of minutes? Wasn't our talking cure, then, rather like a plumber placing the toilet ten feet from the pipes and hoping that enough of the discharge would reach its mark to fill the municipal cesspools? Why the distance? Why these infinite extensions of space?

The tram ran warm and empty, stopping only at my behest. No one else was on the Avenue of Progress. The white façades rose up on either side, pale and perfect in the bright moonlight. The windows up and down the Avenue were lightless, except directly to my right, where the Doctor-General's surgical lamp burned. The snow had long ago been trimmed and packed, iced down and kept away from the sidewalks and road. Even the violence of yesterday's storm had not disturbed the neat squares cut by the ministerial gardeners.

The guard knew me well. He walked me down the broad main hall to the locked door of my Doctor-General's wing. I could hear his small electrical saw worrying its way through some stubborn matter. It purred, raising and lowering the bright lights in the room where he worked by its hungry sucking of power from the wall plug. It was always like Christmas in my Doctor-General's rooms, new gadgets, bright colors splattering his smock, the festive light reflecting crimson and purple and green off the crystalline decanters of liqueur.

"Ah, my friend," he called cheerily. "Make yourself at home." I sat by the blazing hearth and held my cold hands up to the dancing flames.

"Will we have time tonight to work, inside?" I asked, feeling sheepish about my tremendous need for the inner chamber. The powerful saw obscured my plea, peppering my Doctor-General with a nasty stream of bone chips and debris. He drew the blade away, cursing, and batted his goggles off with a swat of his rubber-gloved hand.

"Damn it," he continued. "Why can't anyone follow orders around here." He threw the dumb mechanical thing against the wall with some force, chipping the elegant wood panel. I kept quiet on my plush footstool, pretending fascination with the billowing flames. Surely he'd be done soon. The desk would be cleared and a copy of the manuscript retrieved so that we might get down to the business at hand. Indeed, already I heard the peeling off of his rubber gloves, the loosening of his smock strings. I turned and peeked.

"Tough night?" I asked tentatively.

"Tough night," he agreed, a low note of sadness in his voice.

"Dull blade?" I guessed.

"Dull mechanic," he spat, venting a small portion of his bile. "I specifically asked for him to set the guide at seven centimeters. Not six, or eight. Seven. Well, you see what he's done," my exasperated counselor added, gesturing at himself to indicate the awful trail the blade shot up his smock and goggles. "I pay a good penny, even for these road kills. Can't afford to be losing them all to human error."

"Sit," I ordered, taking the situation in hand. "Come on now, off with the smock, put it all behind you. Sit, here by the fire." I got up, offering him the little stool. "What can I pour you?" He unburdened himself of the bloody garments.

"Chartreuse, if you would, green Chartreuse." He was a man of sophisticated tastes. I'd known that from the start. He slumped onto the stool, overly tired and grateful.

"You're letting it get to you," I cautioned, taking the firm tone he'd identified as healthiest. "Whose schedule are you running on, anyway? Who's in charge here, after all?" I listened carefully to his silence. Evidently, the questions were rhetorical, so I picked up in his stead. "Do the damn work at your own pace. You're nobody's two-bit yard boy anymore, my Doctor-General." It was strong stuff, but he seemed to need it. He shook his head in agreement, knocking back the small tumbler of Chartreuse manfully, then giving it back to me for more.

"Join me, please," he bade. "I hate to drink alone."

"Lord, uh, yes," I tried (mimicking the tone I'd overheard once in a regular sort of place). "I will, yes, thank you." I poured two more, letting the sticky syrup touch lightly upon the lip of the glass, and scooted onto the bristly velvet stool alongside him.

"To your full recovery," he proposed.

"And yours," I agreed. We touched glasses and tossed them back together.

"What a world," he mused dreamily. "What a fucking world." It was my signal. I cuffed him brutally.

"What a fucking world, guy," I said, beating on his shoulders.

"Another?" he asked, cheered by my easy camaraderie.

"Another, fuck thank you." It wasn't really so difficult, except for this disturbing urge in my groin. He filled the tumblers full again and raised his glass to mine.

"To the Prime Minister," he roused patriotically.

"The Prime Minister," I answered with sincere enthusiasm. "His full recovery." We tossed them back again, spilling only a little before refilling (the Doctor-General having taken over the decanter).

"Your turn," he said, licking the sweet green dribble from his chin. "Make it good, guy." He swatted me, and I him.

"To the time of melting," I burst out, knowing I meant it. "Hurry it up the fuck."

"The fuck up," he agreed, tipping the bottle into his mouth. We sat in our warm, brief buddydom, tousling each other's hairs appreciatively, giggling into the dwindling green supply, while our thoughts drifted, unspoken, by the fire. Luckily, my more experienced mate took the lead.

"Look, my man," he counseled, evidently aborting our brief revel. "All's well and good and all, but I've got a report to do, and pronto, yard boy or no." He staggered back toward the bloody table. "And you can help."

"Ah, yes, the manuscript." I was eager. A little aperitif never hurt me as a reader. In fact, I felt rather sharpened than dull, my nimble mind loosened by the few nourishing sips I'd taken. "Let me have it," I suggested. Strangely, he pulled his smock back on.

"Not that, you boob," he laughed, still batting me about as though our buddydom was some sort of permanent condition. "Up on the table. I've got to get some photos for the report."

"Photos? Photos of what?"

"Your brain, my man, documentation. I can't very well send in my report without it." He smiled generously, as if this opportunity were a gift for which I should be grateful.

"X-ray photos?" I asked, still unwilling to believe.

"Nope."

"Well, my Doctor-General. I mean, I can't very well believe that you wish to cut my head open, I . . . You yourself said it may be months yet." The full range and feeling of my objections defied speech. It's not that I would ever hesitate to allow him this opportunity, once he'd worked the bugs out. But now, when I knew him still to be striking the vertebral arteries of helpless cadavers with his clumsy knife, I'd certainly put my foot down in defense of my head. He hovered close, wrapping an arm around me as reassurance.

"Now, now, my friend. You do surprise me. Have I ever endangered you, or your head?" My silence said go on. "Have I ever attempted to hide the occasional glitches in my new technique?" At this I nodded no. In fact he'd always been quite forthcoming about it. "And haven't we both agreed that, when I'm ready, if you wish, and only if you wish, we'll let you be the first to benefit from the new miracle surgeries?"

"Well, yes, my Doctor-General, and in fact I may want very much to be so blessed. But not prematurely. Why, just look at your smock. Look, look at what has happened, not twenty minutes ago while I sat here by this very fire." I implored him with my eyes to understand this subtlety—that while I blanched now, I would not hesitate to support him in the ripeness of his project.

"But I wasn't proposing surgery tonight. Just some photos."

"But, Doctor, photos of my brain you said. How on earth do you propose to make it visible?"

"A small deception, I guess. We need merely to make it *look* like your brain. Thus the pig." He gestured to the unmoving, once-pink thing into whose cranium he'd earlier been sawing. "If you'll just pose as the patient, I believe I can arrange the site artfully enough. The pig's brain should be a plausible stand-in for your own. It won't take but an hour or two." He clapped me again on the back, as if to seal the deal. "Besides," he concluded, "you really don't have a choice."

The Doctor-General had me undress and slip into a hospital gown. My head was wrapped in cotton gauze, with a plastic breathing apparatus stuffed into my mouth. He'd left the top of my head exposed and I was surprised when, a few minutes into the procedure, I felt warm liquid flowing freely over my scalp. It would've raised a small panic had I not heard the sound of water running. Water. It was water, warm and ample, dripping through my hair delightfully. I could've been at the barber, so comforting was this small amenity.

"Are you washing my hair?" I mumbled through the decoy tube.

"Uh, yes I am. Just part of my usual service. Nothing's too good for my patients, after all." He hummed contentedly. The steel snap of cutting shears sounded above me, and I felt him pull gently at my hair.

"What now, Doctor, what's going on out there?"

"I'm cutting the hair, making it shorter." He snipped close to my scalp, letting the cool breeze brace me where, as far back as I could remember, I had never before been braced.

"But why, Doctor? And why are you cutting it so short?"

"Short? Why, you'll have no hair at all in just a minute." I smelled the soapy shave cream, its aroma loosed by my Doctor-General's vigorous working of the brush and cup. It felt queer on my bare head, all tingly and suffocating at once. I wished my hands had not been put in the restraints so that I might touch the tiny bristles before they were swept away under the passing of the blade. But it was no use. The tube turned speech into a tiring and futile gesture. He really was quite good at this, I had to admit. It was worth getting past my resentment, simply so I could lay back and enjoy the shave. The blade passed over my scalp with swiftness and subtlety, easily sweeping the tender surface clean.

I sighed and waited. I couldn't see through the bandages, but I heard the liquid suck of the cranial cavity as he lifted the pig's brain out. Would mine sound that way? Perhaps my cavity was deeper and would elicit a more vibrant, throaty sound? If one could use a local anesthetic, leaving the connections largely intact, it might be possible to listen to the sound of one's own brain being lifted from its pan. That would be a treat. He placed the pig's brain down, swearing at his own incompetence for having forgotten the marking of the lines. I felt the neat tip of the marker work its way from front to back, tracing the parallel borders of the flap he would pull back. Perhaps it was all a therapeutic ruse, readying me for the actual operation by conducting a mock-up early on? He turned the bright lights on full and snapped a quick series of photos: stage one.

Now he sliced the surface of the pig's brain as thinly as he could and laid it over my scalp. I doubt I'll ever experience such a thing again. Then came the constructing of the wound (bone, flap, etc.). It was a challenge beyond even the most senior of the Salon staff, and I envied my Doctor-General the opportunity to undertake so daring and paradoxical a cosmetic surgery. Imagine, a mask made to reveal the interior. He'd not gotten to be a Doctor-General simply for his stupidity and sloth. I've seen the photos; that man is no slouch.

He was true to his promise and had me unwrapped and washed before the hour struck ten. He sawed the animal up and stuffed it in trash bags, not wanting there to be any suspicion of wrongdoing. Science is a fickle mistress. My Doctor-General had even arranged a realistic hairpiece to replace my fallen locks. I tried it on, admiring its fit and styling, before slipping back into my clothes and settling by the fire (uncertain whether he still meant to take us over the threshold tonight).

Did he wonder, too (wiping the blood from his hands by the icy black windows), after the manner in which the heavens hung above us? Had he ever imagined himself a bird brushing at the edge of the sphere, his wing breaking the brittle shell, or wondered how it was possible his thought could stretch so far as to encompass everything, the totality held within his head as if within the final invisible film? And had he trouble, too, with the division between that expansive thought and "him," he who was contained inside his body, trapped within its own fragile shell? Oh, I was filled to bursting with my curiosities (forever unspoken) about the boundaries that kept us apart. Kiss me, I thought, dwelling more on the epistemological than on the erotic implications of that intermingling. Those bare, rock islands gave us containers far more constricting and invisible than the crystalline spheres.

"Will we?" I asked meekly, unable to utter the sacred name. The nod of my head and timid gesturing of my eyebrows told him what I meant: the inner sanctum. My Doctor-General stared into the night for some moments before turning toward me and walking near. The news he had to deliver was not good.

"I must be frank," he began. "I feel it's time I confronted you about an issue, something which might be acting to impede your progress toward recovery." He patted my shoulder with his bloody hand. "I fear I have been remiss, simply hoping the issue would work itself out without our confronting it directly."

"My Doctor-General, don't blame yourself."

"No, no, please. I'm not blaming anyone. In fact, I don't want to talk to you about it now."

"But, I . . . " It was still unclear to which "it" (among my myriad transgressions) he was referring.

"We'll not be going in tonight, you see. I'd like to get to this on some evening when we're not so fagged by the late hour and our labors." My heart sank. "And I'd like to ask you to do something for me." Read his paper, at last? "I want us to take ten days apart, to give us time for independent reflection, let the tide of life sweep over us just a bit, get a fix on things. And I'd like you to use that time, my friend, to clarify two things. Think about your goals, what you imagine will be the end point of our therapy. I want you to think about this quite specifically, jotting down, perhaps a, what do you writers call it, a . . . "

"A treatment?"

"A scenario. A scenario describing our last session together. Can you do it?"

"Our last, ever?"

"Yes, exactly." It sounded so apocalyptic.

"What's the other thing you wanted me to clarify?"

"I want you to think about Dexter. You never speak of him, or rarely. Think about his life now, what you imagine he's doing, or feeling. You needn't write it down yet, just be ready to talk and listen next time."

"Ten days?" Could it be true? As suddenly as that everyone was leaving me.

"Ten days, half-past seven again."

The cold evening was empty, the broad Avenue silent, and I walked to the seawall, considering the layers which my Doctor-General now sought to unravel. Pale frozen waves broke against the wall, lacing the rough stones with ice. I drank the air through my thin muffler, marveling at the black sky from whence it poured. How enormous I seemed, just then, extending beyond the sliver moon to a totality so broad and encompassing that no measure could possibly contain me. I paused for a moment, then collapsed back into myself.

How often I'd tried to *think* my way inside, pursuing the same course the knife desired, but with the incisive thought. I could travel in through my eye, the vision of Hakan's soft flat belly, perhaps, carrying me with it. The symmetry of his muscles there, and the shallow belly button. This vision, this thought, rushing along the optic nerve on its way inside, would trip every signal in turn, and arrive, finally, at my special sensitivity (somewhere behind my face). The Doctor's glinting knife can be seen scraping clumsily through flesh, swinging this way and that, in search of the *same* location to which the vision of Hakan took me with such greater swiftness and surety. He slashes and cuts, the blade worrying its way blindly through pieces of brain. Will he ever find me?

What genius peeled the flaps of my skin back to uncover a pig brain? What would he find were he to dig further, wiggling the knife that extra inch? Was Dexter trapped inside? It could be so, his image and smell so persistent within me. The ocean kept tilting at the shore, running up into my shoes, catching the moon's thin light in a salty drop on my eyelash. Really, his image had dimmed in the passing weeks, wed to or obscured by the athletic form of Hakan. But Dexter. My Doctor-General had pointed me back to Dexter.

It was true, I rarely mentioned him, though he'd never really left my mind. I sometimes imagined him in his little bedroom, lying on the floor with a book and all the pillows (as he was wont to do). I wished vainly he would write me, or at least miss me, as I truly missed him. The Doctor-General had warned me against contacting him, and I was good to my word. Perhaps Dexter received similar warnings? Sometimes I despaired of his ever remembering our love and how much he had meant to me. Maybe he already had another boyfriend. I knew he wouldn't be wanting for suitors. But so long as he missed me, I would always love him.

His life had gone on. He flourished, no doubt, still at the top of his class, the funny, lovable boy whose sensitivity everyone sensed and cherished. I only wished that I could be with him through all that lay ahead. It was a queer sadness, at once proud and lonely, wronged and self-righteous. I should have been his lover for all our lives, but now that was over and I could only love him inside my heart.

I was wandering through the narrow streets paying scant attention to my progress or direction. Evidently, some internal compass was at work, and I looked up from my memories to see the closed wooden door of the Burlesque. Odd, it was just before midnight. The first or second show should have been underway, towering bitches staggering in or out of the portal. I could hear nothing, not even a peep from behind the blank door. I stepped carefully down, bracing myself against the stones, and tried my strength against the barrier. Nothing. It didn't give. Had the snows proven to be too much? The Burlesque had run every night for almost a decade now, triumphant over hurricanes, blizzards, and twisters. I knocked loudly against the standards but to no avail. Nothing. I turned away, toward home and bed.

The sunlight came to my window, surpassing the close and crowded buildings across the lane. It dappled my room in a motley of shadows and light. I lay among the bedclothes, wondering about my Doctor-General's predilection for green Chartreuse. It had stayed with me, a sticky sickness in the bottom of my throat. There seemed to be some passage, my spine perhaps, connecting the pit of ill-feeling in my abdomen with a cloudy dullness in the back of my brain.

Ten days. I'd be without my Doctor-General. Hakan was in the hills, not due back, I figured, for at least two or three days. My neighbor and sage was gone, off on his vacation or whatever. I tried to erase the memory of his hanging screws, the torn wood still worming around their teeth. More disturbing than his sudden exodus, however, was the mysterious closure of the Burlesque. I'd seen no signs, no evidence of intervention or governmental action against the patrons or proprietor.

I was to meet the Prime Minister that evening. He had grown impatient in the last weeks, uncomfortable with the prolonged exposure of his skin and uncertain about the prospects of his new face. I was giving him back his cross to bear, fixing it on permanently in the form of his new-old face. It condemned him as it empowered him, making him, once again, our beloved and feared leader. He still had a few weeks of anonymity, however, before the familiar features would take shape. This evening I would see the result of his week of oils—a revitalized skin (I hoped), that could stretch painlessly out to its former fullness. I had a full program of implants and exercises lined up, the final phase in the building of our base, on which I would then erect the new-old face.

I harbored the secret hope that he would be handsome. I wanted his gaze to soothe and reassure me, as my Doctor-General's had. But thus far he'd only been upsetting, both in his speech and appearance. The face itself was so exposed and fragile. His hollow eyes were pits into which I fell. If I made the face healthy, ministering to it with oils and massage, perhaps the eyes would fill up, begin exuding the sort of geometry and organization I felt from the eyes of my Doctor-General. I wanted him, my leader, to command me from a position of strength, not tragedy.

They were a pair, it was true, my Doctor-General and he. Flip sides of a coin, one doctor and one patient to me, one healer and one worrier of wounds. Oh, but the Prime Minister pushed the salt in deep to my open cuts, and without, perhaps, knowing it. Wasn't that my Doctor-General's prescription too, opening the wounds wide, aggravating them with prods and pokes so they might finally heal? And wasn't *he* my patient as much as I was his? My doctor leader, and my leader prone and helpless in the chair? Dearly I wished that either one might coalesce into all these things, replacing the confusion of identities and roles with the simple, single . . . father? friend? image? . . . I needed.

I was alone in the Salon. I slipped into my mask and gown and walked the short distance to the Chamber, closing the door behind me. It was dark here, my arms invisible. Was it possible to make love to Hakan or to Dexter without a body? I sensed an echo of my doctor's inner chamber. The easy darkness let me slip away from earth again, and I wondered if sex could happen between minds. The door was opened and he came in.

"We're alone, Mr. Sludge," he whispered. "I've let myself in." I heard him shuffle toward the chair, bumping a small cart I'd thoughtlessly left standing by the counter. He sighed, overtired from his walk.

"I'm not used to so much walking." I listened to his labored breathing, resting as he lay in the darkness. I remembered my first nights with Dexter, the long hours through which he slept, black and white in the moonlight, the small stuffed animals he still had from childhood crushed beside the bed. We hadn't noticed them in our passion. I lay beside him, propped up on my elbow, watching him breathe. He was feverish, his eyes turned back into private dreams. The Prime Minister had fallen asleep. His breathing shifted into his nose, dragging heartily across the phlegm.

What a difficult, unprecedented change he was undergoing. Had anyone before lost so public and permanent a face as his? Had they then suffered a resurrection, a recommencing of their sacrifice by voluntary recovery? I understood his exhaustion, both spiritual and physical. The strain of recovery could be too much, sometimes, even for a younger man.

"Oh, ah," he started, gasping suddenly. "Mary, God, oh Deb." His fit diminished into sighs and then even breathing. He woke, apparently undisturbed by this fragmentary outburst. "I believe I'm ready for you now, if you wish."

I engaged the small desk lamp, pointing its light toward the wall. He yawned and rubbed the sleep from his face with both hands. It was a good sign, his vigorous rubbing.

"How does your face feel?"

"It tingles, still. I don't dare turn it toward anyone. I feel as though my skull's been exposed." The tingling was good, the healthy response of living skin. He'd have to deal with his shame and embarrassment.

"Are you ready for the bright lights?" I touched him softly on the cheek.

"Yes." I pressed the two buttons, bringing the lights powerfully to life. The Prime Minister shaded his eyes, letting the shadow of his hand fall across his face. The skin was beautiful. It was pale and still milky, but imbued with a deep glow of life. There was depth and substance in flesh which last week had seemed as thin as parchment.

"It's really quite impressive. I'd guess you're the envy of all the ladies. May I?" I offered up both my hands for a thorough feel.

"Uh, yes, of course," he answered. "I do hope you're not making a cruel joke about the ladies."

"Mr. Prime Minister, in all frankness, this is the most astonishing skin I've ever worked with. It's as soft as a child's bottom, sir. Haven't you seen it yourself?"

"No." He answered with gruff honesty. "And I can't say that I intend to." Immediately, not bothering this time to ask or cajole, I picked up the big hand mirror and held it in front of him.

"Look, look at it." I pressed the mirror into his shaky grip, shaming him into using it. "Nothing to be frightened of, simply skin, beautiful new skin." He took a small peek, grimacing and blinking as though looking into a bright light. "I've done a creditable job I'd say." He looked again, touching his face as he surveyed it.

"It's not so awful," he allowed. He inspected it openly now, stretching and turning to see its various phases, trying out a small handful of expressions. "I'd not think it freakish, really, if I saw it."

"In one week, you'll even wish you weren't going ahead with a new face, I can promise you." This brought a cynical laugh.

"I have no intention of becoming some sort of circus freak."

"Mr. Prime Minister, be ready, then, to be amazed. One week. You've got to keep heart, sir, no matter what doubts you harbor."

"I've got a fleet of them, Mr. Sludge, doubts to spare."

"Keep them if you must, but promise me you'll not shirk the exercises I set, not miss a treatment or soak, simply because of your pessimism. Our success depends on it."

I scribbled some final notes on the list I'd written up, packing it in his kit with the oils and salves. "The instructions are quite explicit. You can call me if there's anything wrong, anything I've left unclear." Hope coursed through me like parental affection, alternately raising kindness and severity in my manner toward him. When, at last, I sent him out into the sparkling night, I watched his big back wobble away into the dark, the small box swinging slightly in his grip. Therein he held his future, among the oils and ablutions that were all I could provide.

Oh, how queer to be alone, the shank of the evening stretched out before me, with no prospect of Hakan returning to comfort me in my bed. I relished the air, its softness and promise. Water was seen to drip from the crooked stalactites of ice; my breath clouded gently without freezing into crystal. Hakan's breath mingled with it, mixing with mine in every mouthful. We mingled in the mouth of my father, unthinking by his wireless, letting slip a bit of air in through his thin nostrils; we mingled in Lucrezia, her broad lungs drawing whole acres of air. We were dancing together in every cloud. How could he be lost, his breath so ever-present, violating my every pore? What had he touched inside me that I came so swiftly to love him? Habitually, I traced it back to Flessinger and Ponz, the terrible genius of their device.

Had it any parallel in Dexter, this delightful love? I had never thought to wonder, except now that my Doctor-General directed me that way. Dexter. My hunger for him was so tender and sad. We were tangled together by need, swallowed by each other both at once, until, well. I had no sense of need from Hakan. His joy nourished me and destroyed any confidence I had about the nature of our connection. If it wasn't frightening, if it didn't yawn open like a chasm, was it really love? The Prime Minister's confessions echoed inside me: he knew love as I did, a terrible consuming thing, our destiny and doom.

My hunger for Dexter was a pain I would always welcome. But I could not reconcile my twin emotions, this true and utter love for Dexter and my complete joy in the sensual delights of the rebel boyfriend Hakan. I sighed deeply, tasting in the air the mingled breath of both these divinities. I imagined them, tangled together in their muscular exertions, sprawled across one another's bodies. It consoled me, this thought. Love might never answer to the demands of reason, nor my Doctor-General.

Hakan arrived, in his fashion, late in the ever-warmer week. He beamed his delight at my welcome, stripping off his clothes with impatience, and wrapped me inside his laughing limbs. He was an overload of stimulations, tripping over every word in his eagerness to tell me what his comrades had concluded about the mysterious letter. He smiled with the pleasure of what he'd found out. "It's him, you see, everyone says it's him actually. The neighbor of yours was very big from way back. He will be smuggling our leader, disguised as the Prime Minister, remember?"

"He'll be smuggling who?"

"Scheeperleider. This 'Scheeperleider' *is* the opposition leader. He's coming here disguised as his old opponent, the Prime Minister. Just like in the letter, 'I am again him, or me. The opposite.' He'll be on a ship for the Festival of Melting."

"Why?" I asked vaguely. "I mean, why should he dress as the Prime Minister?" And wouldn't the Prime Minister be dressing as himself too? (If I finished his new face on time.)

"So he'll *be* the Prime Minister, you see, and maybe take power without even a fight. It's hard to tell if that sort of deception will even work; who can know? The face might be completely wrong." Right or wrong, he probably looked a good deal *more* like the Prime Minister than the Prime Minister (at this point in time).

"There won't be fighting, will there?" I stroked his tender skin, there above his heart where a blade might easily rip through.

"Well, not if this works, or if we can rally support behind him and Lucrezia."

"Lucrezia?"

"They say she is involved."

"The Burlesque has been dark," I told him. "Ever since the lobster man disappeared."

"Your neighbor?"

"Yes, the day you left. I stopped by that night, and there was nothing, nobody."

"Well, there it is, obviously. She's in hiding, getting ready."

He rolled over on top of me, whispering his excitement into my ear. "We'll be watching the harbor for him. They say two Dutch ships are due this week, and another a week from now. Lucrezia and, and . . . "

"The lobster man," I mumbled into his warm, blushing face.

"The lobster man. They're going to board the ship and smuggle him in."

"And what will *you* do, my angel? Will we be together?" I squeezed him and wondered about our future in these tumultuous times.

"Every minute," he said. "We're to watch the harbor, together."

Had I asked him to stay? I mean, forever?

* * *

The days became warmer still. If this condition lingered, we might be in the midst of melting, and revolution, within a week. Really, I didn't believe it, even then. The rebels weren't capable of such violence or guile as it would take. Even my unwavering devotion to Lucrezia couldn't blind me to that fact. No one *really* wanted change. I hadn't thought the rebels were even interested in it. It was such a threat to their position as rebels. Fail or succeed, such actions as were now proposed would end forever their status. They were "the opposition" and nothing else. What else could they possibly be?

Hakan went to the kitchen for tea. "I'll not have to question the Prime Minister now, will I?" I called to him. The cloud of politics seemed to promise at least this silver lining. He poked his tousled head back through the doorway.

"No, I don't think you will."

"Nothing, really, except to help you watch the harbor, isn't that so?"

He paused. "Nothing much. Nothing at all, actually."

His clarifications unnerved me. "Nothing?"

"No," he said. "Nothing, nothing at all. You are not to finish his new face."

"What?"

"No face. The Prime Minister cannot have his face if we are to succeed."

"But my work, my preparations." He returned and kissed me (a tactic which had worked well enough before). "Couldn't I just finish it and then undo it?" I asked.

"No. It's not even for us to say."

"It's certainly for me to say, though, isn't it?" I was weary of his bossy ways. "I'll just have to decide what's what and what isn't." He returned to the kitchen, then came back, plying me with tea.

"Think of him a minute. There cannot be *two* Prime Ministers. If you give him his face, one will die, maybe him. Without his face, he goes away. No one recognizes him. He slips back into life, and our new leader has his place. You see, if you want his blood on your hands, go ahead, give him his face."

"But how do they know he's coming back as the Prime Minister?" I was grasping at straws and he knew it. He simply nodded no again.

"I'll be seeing him, in two nights," I reported mournfully.

"That's fine," Hakan whispered, "that's fine. You should go on as if nothing is changed. You simply won't be finishing."

"Just as if nothing was different? Prepare the parts, lay the base?"

"Yes," he acknowledged. "Every step, just as you have normally done it, except you don't give him the face."

"Let me hold you, my people, in my armory," I remember the Prime Minister had once said, hoping to articulate clearly the utter completeness of his affections. He stood upon the winter dais (it must've been years ago) facing the glowering storm, a curious mole on his upper lip. The leader seemed energized by the intensity of the weather. "You be quiet," he scolded, quelling an unwelcomed interruption. His arm extended, he pointed an accusing finger at the one obstreperous nun, explaining "this is a democracy we're running here. I have a right to speak." We voiced our agreement with spontaneous cheers.

"Let me hold you, my people," he repeated, incantatory, "in my armory." His voice echoed off the gathered throng, booming into the bright, electrical air. A silken smock extended behind his head, folded over and supported on ivory stakes above him. It formed a little shelter against the slashing rain. His long tresses had been braided and hung in a bright golden snood.

I was just one of the multitudes, gathered in obeisance to our leader, attracted, too, by the pageantry of the melting. Had he reached down to touch me, passing his tender hands across my brow? It felt so, his corpus so soft and animated, affirming for all who'd come to see that his was no photographic illusion, his illusion was real. Sometimes you simply become what other people say you are. Certainly we did, formed like warm putty into the shape of his rhetoric. We became what he spoke. Virtuous, resolute, pious, and just. We, the people, cheered for the picture he painted of us. As though a Doctor-General to us all, he wrapped our fluid souls in a firm and binding silk, giving us a particular shape and identity.

Phrases were repeated in the news, examples culled from the ministerial archives, further illustrating the sort of persons we were. Later polls would be taken, testing our powers of recall, a last quiz to see if we'd remembered our identity in all its subtlety. Would we stand for injustice? No! Was our people a generous people? Yes!

Could it ever be so good without him? I wondered, melancholy, what our new changes would bring.

We sat beside the ramparts, our backs against the warm stone, gazing out into the harbor through a pair of lenses provided by the rebels. It was innocent enough, two bird-watchers or lovers of the bay. Two mild afternoons had passed thusly, accompanied by our plentiful picnic hamper and a camera designed to attach easily to the powerful lenses. Nothing had been seen. Two ships flying the Dutch tricolor had set anchor, sitting among the foreign vessels that filled the busy waterway. We kept watch over the infrequent activity of their decks. My young rebel boyfriend was irrepressible, glowing with anticipation. Not so me. Though not glum, I lay upon our blankets steady, still, and quiet, affecting an attitude of deep reflection. Hakan showed some patience and understanding, taking care not to mention him, the one whose face I was constructing. I winced, occasionally, at the pain. The thought of him undone hurt me in my soul.

"Maybe we should hire a boat," Hakan said, the lenses pressed to his face. "You know, go out at night and try to get on board." I lay beside him, gazing along the line of his view, watching the untroubled harbor. Students strolled through the melting snows, let out from lectures and libraries for this hour or two of lunch.

"Oh, I don't think so." Action of any sort seemed dangerous and unnecessary. I didn't mind our picnic days, nor our creepings about the waterfront at night. But they were both quite legal. "It's a great risk, if we're caught." We had a particular task to carry out, and even my impatient boyfriend had to accept that. He put the lenses down and turned to me, bunching my muffler up warmly to my chin.

"No, you're right," he sighed. "I'm no good at waiting."

"No, you're not," I agreed. "You're very impatient sometimes."

"Well, yes. You were too, right? When you were my age?" I blushed, touched by his interest.

"I suppose." Was I? Had I been? To my best powers of recollection, no. I'd been turned so completely inward at that age . . . I had nothing to be impatient with. Everything that mattered to me took place inside, existing only in that private interior space where no outside measure of time could be brought to bear. "No," I said at last. "I guess I wasn't."

"No?" He laughed, taking my confession as a ruse. How much I wished it had been so, wanting to have at some point been what I knew him to be—passionate and young, impatient with the chaotic course of worldly events. I wanted to have cared enough to be troubled by the world around me. "You were always grown-up? I think you're not remembering well." He was, sadly, wrong. I'd not always been grown-up, but I'd always been something quite other than what he was now.

"No, I remember. I never cared about things so strongly as you." Now he blushed. I always thought of *him*, no matter what he asked of me. Love remade the world, revealing him in every part of it. Perhaps this same force impelled my Doctor-General to turn all *his* inquiries back upon *me*.

"You care about Lucrezia."

"It's not the same." I knew he was only guessing.

"You care about me." Now we both blushed. I looked at the blustery sky, wondering if I would've cared so much had I met him in my youth. I probably had, that is, met someone very much like him. One of the boys, probably, who'd been kicked out of school. I despised them then, thinking them gross and uncultured. Could any of them have shared the divinity that imbued him, Hakan, my rebel boyfriend? I was so blind and helpless. Perhaps my deepest passion was merely the product of Flessinger and Ponz. It shamed me to think so. I said nothing, and felt the sadness well up inside me, warming my eyes. Hakan, innocent, took my tears simply as evidence of affection.

The evening brought back a trace of winter. The black sky stirred with brutal winds, frozen blasts that whistled past the church spires, digging down into the streets at will. Hakan and I wobbled uncertainly toward the docks, wrapped in our mufflers and heavy sweaters, hoping to make the acquaintance of anyone who might know something of the ships, still at anchor on the bay. I kept my arm across Hakan's slim shoulders to steady us both. The hill dropped steeply down, and we slid the last hundred yards as if on fishmongers' slabs.

The docks by night were a far different purlieu than by day. The noise and clamor of commerce was silenced. Cranes loomed empty overhead, their gears halted. Cables swung loose, slapping in the winds. You could look up and down the length of the over-built piers and see no one until you looked again. The tiny glow of a cigarette tip, another. An empty can tipped over by accident, the drunken stumbler clattering into the alleyway. Shadows, then light when the shadow moved on. Up and down the waterfront, an evening community was carrying on its own commerce, as vital to the docks as the business of the day.

It was Hakan who first spotted him, an old man uncomfortably similar in shape and posture to my crustaceous ex-neighbor. He'd been standing quite near us for some time, quietly drawing on his pipe; the ember was hidden by his cupped hand. I hadn't even seen him when Hakan, ever the bold one, stepped confidently into the shadows and extended a hand and a whispered greeting. A draw on the exposed pipe revealed them both in its orange glow. I couldn't hear exactly what was said. Within a minute they'd parted.

"He knows," Hakan whispered, steering me away from the docks, toward the hill. "He's been told by the Dutch that Scheeperleider's on the next ship."

"He's not Scheeperleider?" I asked.

"No, of course not." Hakan laughed at my ignorance. "He's our contact, knows the docks."

We kept near the wall, steadying ourselves against the wind, testing each footstep along the pavement. "When is this ship due, anyway?"

"We don't know. There are sailors who can tell us, but our man has no contact with them. That's where we're going now, to find these guys." I held on to his arm, following him toward this impulsive rendezvous.

The Dutch dinghy bobbed in the water, disgorging a small clutch of sailors to shore. They'd come to port, apparently, for an evening's revel. Hakan, with customary boldness, intercepted them and offered himself as a willing guide to the city's charms and entertainments.

They were gangly and young, one almost as tender in his years as Hakan, the other two barely into their twenties. They spoke a surpassing English, and seemed quite unlike the brawling, brutish sailors in my pirate books. I found myself charmed into liking them.

"You've missed the best show," Hakan told them, boasting. "Lucrezia. It's a shame." The little tart. Had he ever even seen her? And yet he presumed, speaking as if familiar. I swallowed my objections, tweaking his blushing ear with a soft finger, and grimaced my complaint to him.

The Dutchmen, it turned out, wanted nothing more than a nice café in which to sit and talk to us about our city. They were a fine and civilized bunch. I'd expected drunken brawls and trips to brothels, a run-in, perhaps, with the Parks Rangers. What a marvelous school system they must have, I thought, to produce such inquisitive and cultured youths even among their sailors.

"Perhaps the Eichelberger," I proposed. "An older café on the prettiest of our central squares." We caught the tram toward the opera house.

Rattled and rumbled in my seat, I watched our bright reflections in the black glass of the tram window. Had I ever imagined that I might some day ride a midnight tram, with my Mediterranean rebel boyfriend by my side, planning the secret interrogation of an innocent trio of Dutch sailors? Certainly I had not. Nor could I have anticipated the dizzying permutations of love through which I'd been thrust by the impelling force of the Criminal and Health systems. What marvels I had found in this my new-new life. I brushed my hand across Hakan's warm cheek, wondering at the roots of my desire and shame. If only we had met in school, or camp. Somewhere, anyway, where I had models available—a role to play, confidence in the clear expressions of my soul. I drifted away, achieving an immeasurable distance from which remove I viewed the rest of this troubling evening.

*   *   *

"Have you good football here, in your city?" the youngest one asked as we gathered around one of the larger tables. Miss Eichelberger fawned over my guests as if they were her own children.

"Soccer football?" Hakan inquired, the expert on all things. "Or rugby football? We've only got rugby football you see, though some schools have soccer." A dull but impassioned discussion followed concerning the relative value of the two sports, each side maintaining a greater interest in the sport of the other. My attention drifted and I smiled ambiguously at the myriad youthful topics they pursued. Examinations, social clubs, sports, and music. I amused myself with communications to Miss Ethyl, trippings of the tongue and tossings of the eyebrow, etc. (deftly deployed from my station toward her, at every far corner of the café). It delighted her, and kept the long train of aperitifs coming with our coffees for the hours we sat and chatted.

"We thought he might have come on one of your boats," I, at one late point, heard Hakan saying.

"Scheeperleider?" the young one asked, laughing. "I have a brother sailing on the next ship, has told me of him in a letter."

"The next ship?" Hakan asked. How on earth had he managed to find the right sailor? It was one of the mysterious powers of the rebels, their deftly accurate intelligence. I had no idea under what ruse Hakan had raised this topic, so I feigned disinterest but kept one ear turned toward them.

"Yeah, yeah, the next that is coming from Holland."

The next ship. Due in five days and, if this young lad could be trusted, carrying Scheeperleider along with it . . . Had my lobster man left our city to join the returning rebel on board? Was he in hiding, readying the ruse that would get this man to land and the Festival of Melting? My four companions babbled into the evening, and I finally rose and begged to take my leave.

"I really must rest, my age, you see." I coughed lightly for effect. "I'll be working tomorrow." I looked toward my young friend, bidding him with my eyes to come. He looked away, and asked the Dutchmen if they had time to see more. "Well, good night then," I finished, taking my hat and scarf and leaving them.

It was all, perhaps . . . real—Hakan's bright fantasy of power changing hands. How arcane it seemed to me, an issue of so little interest and unclear consequence. How could he offer his life to a cause such as this? I understood the love of pageantry. I even shared his fascination with images of power, the symbols by which it is granted or displayed . . . but to expend one's energy on these subtle and boring machinations? It seemed an absurdity, an anachronism in this time of smoothly run democracy. Each and every one of us had our part in the elaborate machine of culture, its wheels and gears turning round and round. Even the rebels had their role. Against what could they be rebelling?

I sat on the empty bed, flipping my resentment around, trying for the root of it. I wanted to pull it clean out and let my loving mind return rightly to Hakan, sainted, flawed teenager. I took the little picture he'd given me from my wallet. The opposition leader. He looked ever more familiar (perhaps because of the frequency with which I pulled the photo out now). I envied this man on a number of vague, confused counts. I envied that Hakan should love him so. He had never asked for a picture of me. I envied the fact of our anticipations of him, our vigil by the ramparts. I envied the intensity of Hakan's enthusiasm at the prospect of his coming. It was late. Alone, I curled around my wallet picture, pressing my face to Hakan's old shoe, the one he'd left lying by the bedside, and fell deep into sleep.

* * *

The Chamber was dark and silent again, the Salon empty. Spring was near enough that the men were away for site work. With the Festival approaching, ministers and their ambitious subordinates remained under cover, preparing the season's new faces. Our staff was stretched to its limit, the artisans ferried about in cabs, tending to their cloistered patrons. I was to produce the centerpiece, the crystal through which all other forms would be viewed, the measuring rod.

Or so it was believed . . . And by whom? Had Doctor Cotton been told? Who else on the staff was working with him? How much did they know, or know that I knew? I dared not share any of my contacts and conversations with them, fearing some violation of protocol, or worse, violence. It lurked now, haunting me by its possibility. What role would there be for the gun and the knife in a week, in ten days, whenever the time for turning came and Lucrezia marched on the city with her leader in tow?

I scratched and stretched, uncomfortable in my skin. The door slipped open. He walked in. My mouth was dry, crowded with the unspoken words of my confession.

"I'm ready, Mr. Sludge," he whispered hoarsely. "You may turn the lights on."

I went to the door and pressed the heavy buttons, watching the merciless light fill the room. He sat still, staring at me, a darkened form (for my eyes had not adjusted). I rubbed them, looked down at the floor for a moment, and then looked up again. It was frightening, and remarkable.

The intervening week indeed had filled his face out completely. It had returned to the shape and heft it sported in its first life. The skin was still soft and supple, enriched by new color, pink with health and blush, ruddy where he'd let the sun touch it. And I recognized him now.

It was him, he whose picture Hakan carried in his heart, the opposition leader.

He sat before me, his difficult life masquerading as the Prime Minister briefly interrupted by the death of his artisan—now awaiting the placement of a new face to hide, again, who he was. The falling death had been faked from a balloon. I looked quickly down again, rubbing my eyes as if they were still blinded, and excused my difficult pause.

"I'm sorry, sir, I, it's these damned lights." Who waited now, I wondered, off our coast, in league with the lobster man? Indeed, the opposition leader was already in power. I turned back toward him, my tools and rag in hand, and smiled a bright smile of appreciation at his healthy face.

"Fine work, sir, I'm proud."

"Is it that bad, Mr. Sludge? Why, you look as though you'd seen a ghost." I chuckled at his joke, mashing his skin between my strong fingers.

"No, sir, not at all. I'm proud. You've obviously followed my instructions to the letter." I took another deep breath and covered his face with a towel, turning back to the counter to compose myself.

"Yes, I did, I'm quite impatient to be done with all this. Spring seems to have come early, you know."

"I know, sir, the time of the melting."

"Will we be ready in time?" he asked, scratching his nose through the towel. "I really can't have them delay the Festival, you see."

I hesitated, coughed, and swallowed. I'd gone ahead and put the parts together, as Hakan had said, proceeding as though all of it eventually would be done. They lay in a box, ready. I could put them on this very moment if I'd a mind to. They would not last unless I laid down a good base (a week's work, maybe less). But they could be worn by him at any point.

"I don't know, sir," I said, choking a bit on the words. "I'm still unsure, what, how, that is, to proceed."

"I'm not a patient man, my friend. I said for the Festival, and for the Festival it shall be."

"Of course it will. I'm just thinking about your health, sir, your well-being. I'll need a decent base to work on, and we're almost there." I spun the gauze neatly from its roll and started wrapping the fresh face he'd shown me. "You'll be under gauze for a few days, nothing severe. I can leave holes for your eyes and mouth, but I've got to get that skin under wraps, at least until Thursday."

"Three days?" he objected, batting at my swift and certain wrapping. "Must it be so long?"

"Three days, Mr. Prime Minister, no less. You're working with the best, sir. It could mean your life."

And yet, in the clarity and light of the following afternoon, we stood against the ramparts and watched for the imminent arrival of the H.K.S. *Oliebollen*, the junk freighter on which the mysterious Scheeperleider was said to be riding. My troubling discovery remained a secret, guarded and kept close to my heart. Hakan lionized the man so. What betrayal he would have felt, the evidence incontrovertibly against him. How beyond his most deeply held political notions was this man's complex blending of competing ideologies. The boy would have been dumbstruck. I doubted that he, or any of the rebels, would see past the appearance of hypocrisy to grasp our leader's genius, his transcendence of all traditional systems of political belief. He was both our leader *and* our opposition leader, our Prime Minister, embodying at once all positions and possible moral values.

Our city required such wisdom of its leader. In the complexity and confusions of our time we relied on the leader, not to advocate particular positions or beliefs, but to animate the *image* of leadership, to bring leadership to life among us. Partisan positions always worked to compromise that pure and higher goal, dragging the leader down into divisiveness and struggle. Our Prime Minister, in his selflessness and genius, recognized our needs and soothed us. He transformed the once rough and solid shape of his positions, erasing them with a solvent of beneficence and lofty dim-wittedness. "Opposition, for, against, reform, tradition." These clumsy words had no place in his lexicon. They were brutal weapons of division and selfishness. In the purity of his vision, our Prime Minister let his old image fall from a balloon and emerged unified, transcendent, our leader.

Hakan was unable to grasp this. Waves of resentment and betrayal would sweep the subtleties away. The child's anger at change would flare into flames, exciting his passion, perhaps stirring him to rash and violent responses. I couldn't risk it, and would not tell him—for his sake, and for the sake of the man whose face and future I still held in my hands.

And so we stood, backs against the rough stone wall, our lenses trained on the entry to the harbor, awaiting the arrival of the imposter expatriate king, "Scheeperleider." Who was this man, and what were his links to my lobster man and Lucrezia? Perhaps he really was (as Hakan had first intimated) mad . . . a crazy old lunatic with a flowing, prodigious pen. The meaning of his mysterious letter was thrown into doubt by my discovery of the identity of our Prime Minister—the Opposition Leader-Leader. What could his baffling claim "I am again him, or me. The opposite," be referring to? Who was he, if now he wasn't he whom we thought, nor, therefore, disguised as he whom we already knew him not to be, that is, the Prime Minister?

Hakan smiled at me breezily, not burdened by the conundrums that spun madly around in my head. I felt the virtue of my silence. My restraint let the boy's enthusiasms remain, alive and uncluttered. Wasn't that an expression of love—my choice to leave him alone, not meddle? Surely it went against all that love had always compelled me toward. But I could feel in the faint glow of that paternal moment a goodness of giving and care in my gesture, a feeling of love for the crooked, unruly flame that burned inside him. I'd let it burn, not fiddling with its elements nor mourning its imperfection.

Perhaps this was the lesson my Doctor-General had saved for me, to love by leaving alone. The message (he had, perhaps, reasoned) would be brought home most forcefully by my remembrance of Dexter, how the little imp had gone on to flourish and thrive without me. It was already soaking into my heart, this bittersweet truth. I took some solace in Dexter's vitality and the beauty of his new life without me, accepting with it the difficult admission that my love and ministrations were not the source of his thriving.

Oh, the bright day beat about me in its blustering chaos. I gazed through canyons of towering clouds emptied of their fury by the season. Sunlight and birds soared along their treacherous faces as the wind blew them over the waters. Much of the snow had melted. Bare patches had come clear in the large public squares, and the roofs all through the old district gleamed wet and clean in the bright sunlight.

Hakan had wandered away, standing dangerously near the precipice that dropped down from the ramparts to the small square below. The powerful lenses were pressed to his face. Out in the harbor I saw it. The gorgeous bright tricolor unfurled in the stiffened breeze. The proud gray bow pointed toward shore. He turned toward me, speechless, his eyes wet with inexpressible joy.

"The ship," he croaked. "He has arrived." The day and its weather converged in a moment of verdant splendor, light cascading from the broken clouds, fixing the ship in its eye, the green waters sparkling all around her. White foam churned in her ample wake. We were dappled in a dancing patchwork of shadows, watching the progress of the Dutch vessel, the *Oliebollen*. Our city welcomed her with its finest profile, the glory of its architecture washed clean and purified by the passage through winter. I could not help but share Hakan's infectious rapture, though I feared the cargo this ship brought to our shore.

It was near dusk, the last hour of our watch, when at last something of significance happened in the harbor. The *Oliebollen* had laid anchor after three, bereft of activity on board until a crew came out to hose down the decks. Hakan thought he'd seen an older man leaning out a portal and vomiting into the sea, but by the time he'd gotten the lenses to me the man had disappeared. By dusk we'd grown weary and lay, half-napping, on our ample blanket. The *Oliebollen* was quiet, deserted it seemed, with only a few lights burning in its cabins. On the far horizon the sun sank out of the clouds and shone briefly, orange and red in its last brilliance, before slipping below the ocean's edge. The harbor's beauty at twilight was stunning. The soft sheet of gray lay liquid and swollen, supporting ships of astounding size and grace. Colorful lights played from their masts, ornamenting the water by their reflections. This vision warmed me; it filled my body with a tenderness that exceeded its cause, touching everything in my purview, particularly the lovely boy Hakan.

A small ship was seen crossing from the docks out into the bay. Hakan raised the lenses to his face, following the path of this tiny vessel. He watched for a short while, grunting his disinterest, then handed the lenses to me.

"It's really strange," he reported. "See what you think."

I trained the powerful instrument on this puzzling craft. It was no larger than a dinghy. A squat old man worked its oars, his amorphous back turned toward us, revealing no clues to his identity. The tall, thin mast wobbled in the wind, useless pulleys and ropes clacking against its brittle length. Rising beside it from where she sat, a woman . . . no, what incredible height . . . and the hairdo.

It was her, resplendent in a fiery tunic and jodhpurs, her shoulders jutting dangerously out below her towering hair. She, Lucrezia, dragging from out of her valise an astonishing dress, iridescent, golden and green and spangled with twinkling sequins, which she fastened to the mast with clothespins and stood by, proudly towering over the harbor, over the city itself. Her banner billowed in the brisk winds, the boatman beating his oars against the waves. I gasped, overwhelmed.

"It's her," I whispered, ever reverent. "Lucrezia."

Hakan took the instrument from my hands and trained it impatiently on her progress, catching, I surmised, his first glimpse of her.

"She's . . . " he started, the words drifting out with awe and disbelief. "She's . . . so tall."

"Yes, she is," I affirmed. "She towers above us all." I lay still in the diminishing twilight, following her distant course across the water, wondering what power could possibly resist her and her mission, whatever it might be.

"And her hair," Hakan continued, betraying his innocence. "I, I've never seen hair like that."

"It's nothing," I offered sagely. "Indoors her hair extends to the rafters, it fairly engulfs you. This is just some little, sensible number, something for an evening in the breeze." I hoped I didn't sound cynical, but my young friend could still not sense the overwhelming dimensions of our beloved Lucrezia. "The dress is sharp, though," I added, looking to help refine his incipient tastes by my example.

"She's so bold, flying it like a banner that way. I wonder what it means?"

As I did. What powers brewed aboard the lumpish *Oliebollen*, that Lucrezia would sail so boldly and triumphantly toward this rendezvous? Surely it was not the rebels, nor any other faction— partisanship could not survive her troubling heights. Whoever was on board that boat, they had not come here as the mouth- piece for some cause. I watched as she clambered up the wobbling rope ladder and was received with salutes and supplication. The Dutch really were a cultured lot. She gave her dress over to the midshipman and stood solemnly. The crew gathered around and watched the running of her colors up the mast. Then she turned toward the city and sang—her song.

O, the glimmering twilight, single stars alight in the dusky sky. Her voice drifted over the open water. I wondered if everywhere the city stopped and turned, eyes searching through the crowded streets, cast beyond the church towers and rooftops, ears captured by that thin, distant sound . . . her song. Recumbent on the warm blanket by the ramparts, I watched her still-distant form. The deaf walls of the university towered behind us. Her song exceeded them, echoing into the hills. Hakan had dropped the clumsy lenses to the ground. He lay beside me mesmerized, his magical eyes fixed on the radiant form standing above the water. I watched him, tears rolling down my face. His little voice whis- pered the words with her, his honey lips mouthing each syllable. He sang, softly, in communion with her, his heart feeling, I thought, the purest element of her passion, teaching him a lesson he might never articulate, nor forget.

* * *

The time had come for my Doctor-General. I'd not managed to fulfill my duties, having ignored the question of "The Last Session," obsessed instead with Dexter. But through that exercise I'd glimpsed what I took to be the lesson he hoped I'd learn—Dexter's independence from me, his thriving without my love. Bittersweet, as I've said, yet a pill that must be swallowed.

He turned and walked silently past me, toward the waiting portal, shedding his stained, surgeon's clothes deliberately at each step. It took my breath from me. He sat down, taking his bag in hand, and slipped it on. I must admit I stared, for the first time violating his blind innocence, letting him believe I too was enbagged. It made me blush and stammer, punishing myself with shame, before finally recovering a measure of respect and slipping my bag on too. The soft cotton slid coolly over my shaven scalp. His wordless intensity told me something severe was in the air, perhaps a lunacy occasioned by the phase of the moon, or some epochal turn in the terms of our relationship.

"Are you quite comfortable?" he asked, beginning.

"Yes, yes I am, Doctor. My scalp feels quite cool against the fabric."

"You have, then, the bag?"

"Yes, I do, I'm wearing it. Are you wearing your bag, Doctor?"

"Yes, I am."

"I looked at you, just now." It made me blush to say it.

"Just now as I sat here?"

"Yes, sir. I hesitated a moment, before putting my bag on, and I saw you, your, your body."

"Was it unpleasant?"

"Why, no, Doctor. I mean, you, you're not unpleasant, per se. I felt bad, though, as I looked, ashamed really."

"Why?"

"I don't know why."

"Surely your feelings have causes."

"I've never noticed, Doctor. Sometimes it's like weather coming in." I sighed deep within the bag. "Why should I feel shame looking at you?"

"Perhaps you were deceiving me."

"I was, yes." He wasn't one to let me off the hook easily. "It made me quite nervous, actually, worrying that you might suspect and catch me at it."

"Why did you want to look?"

"I really don't know, Doctor-General. It's rather like looking at one's mother I suppose, rank curiosity."

"It reminds me of your wanting to ask me questions only a few weeks back. Do you still want to ask questions?"

"No. I fear your answers." Some sort of switch had broken, letting free an uncharacteristic bitterness inside me. "Questions aren't so voyeuristic, are they?" I asked, needling. "You, for instance, my Doctor-General, ask me questions every time. On and on, questions, questions, questions. And you're no voyeur, are you, Doctor-General, I mean, just because you ask me questions?"

"You fear my answers?"

"Yes. Are you or are you not a voyeur, my Doctor-General?"

"I don't understand the question."

"Oh lord in heaven, it's no use. You're just . . . invisible when we're in here." My mind had overheated, running on its own strange motor now. "I only wanted to see that you were here; see you in your nakedness. Will we always be friends, even after I'm better?"

He let slip an uncharacteristic sigh, pausing before he returned to his role. "Would you like us to be friends?"

"Well, I mean, we are friends. And yes, I like being friends, even if it's just therapeutic."

"Do you doubt the sincerity of my friendship?"

"I worry sometimes. I worry you'll just drift away and find a new patient when I get better."

A long and pregnant pause interrupted us. Then my Doctor-General drew a deep breath through his cotton bag.

"Let me get to the point. We've stumbled upon my grave concern simply by pursuing our normal conversation. I mentioned the need for a confrontation and, really, the truth I want you to face begins here. I don't think you sincerely want to get better."

"But of course I do. Haven't I always been willing, eager even, for my treatments? Flessinger, he must have told you."

"But you have never tried to get better."

"I *did* try." His imputations upset me. Hadn't I progressed almost to the third stage in my aversive therapies? And weren't we, he and I, practically drinking buddies now? "Who said I didn't want to get better?"

"You know Flessinger and Ponz were never happy with your progress. Don't deny that. You never made an effort to curtail your erotic responses with them."

"But that's not so, my Doctor-General." I felt like a boy in grade school, falsely accused of plagiarism. "I could hardly be expected, you see. *They*'re the ones who kept showing me films, stimulating me, what with that bag and all. It's not that I didn't try, I did, very much so. And I never ever, you know, twice, and not once with all those horrible bestial films."

"But you did, without fail, respond erotically to the young boy masturbating."

"Well, yes, of course I did."

"Which is the point."

"I'm . . . yes."

"And the poor coach, you really made his job difficult."

"Again, Doctor, the bag, you see."

"Which is why I worry that you've decided you'll be happier if you never get well."

"If I never lose this feeling?"

"Or control it."

"I had . . . my understanding. Aren't I just to act responsibly, my Doctor-General, you know, not hurt anyone?"

"Not have sex with boys."

"Not, yes, I see. Why does the Ministry keep asking me to imagine it then?"

"You seem predisposed against the very foundations on which we've built this program. I hardly expect you to lend an open ear to me, given the confusions in which you're still caught. I don't think you yet accept that sex with boys is not a loving act."

Oh, it struck a knife in my heart, to hear him speak it so plainly. I *had* denied it all along, not wanting ever to see the enormous chasm that separated us, my Doctor-General from me. How could our union ever be complete when such a fundamental issue lay unresolved between us? I'd left it alone all along, sensing, somehow, his inability, his refusal to recognize beauty, to come to terms with that difficult and fragile thing, the love of boys.

"It's so hard to accept, my Doctor-General. How can we, you and I, go on if you insist on this madness?"

"If I insist on what?"

"Perpetrating, coddling this belief that Dexter was not entitled to the fullest expression of my love. How low your opinion of him must be."

"I'm interested in protecting the boy, not depriving him."

"Protecting him from what?"

"From you. The Ministry doesn't simply intervene out of mean-spiritedness, we wouldn't bother if there weren't clear dangers."

"Which were?"

"Your molestations, to begin. We had no reason to believe you capable of self-control. A judgment which, sadly, remains unchanged."

"But we enjoyed sex. We loved it. Doctor, we loved it so much we went ahead and had it, often, despite everything the world had done to make it difficult."

"I'm not interested in listening to you boast about your criminality. Frankly, it saddens me, knowing how miserably I've failed in treating you."

"Oh, it does drive a wedge between us, and I regret that as deeply as you do. Truly I've wanted, as much as you, for our therapy to work its magic. With every day I worry about the progress we've made, wondering when we'll finally move that last step closer to mental health."

"Strangely, I don't doubt your sincerity. I'm just frustrated by the intractable rationalizations you've constructed. It's a fortress, my friend, a fortress of lies within which you hide from the plain truth that sex with boys hurts them. Drivel and gloss all you will about love, you still must accept that unwelcome fact."

"Which lies protect me from it? Help me."

"The belief that Dexter wanted to have sex with you, just to begin."

"He did. He said so, again and again."

"The boy was only twelve. He couldn't possibly know what he wanted, or know what would result from having sex. That's why we have laws, to protect children from being exploited."

"He's a very brave boy, and so full of love. How could I say no after all the courage it took him to ask, to even mention the idea of it?"

"Your embraces were selfish. You would have been acting out of love if you had told him no, if you'd denied the feelings you had for him."

"But then he was delighted, he was ecstatic, beside himself with joy. We weren't hurt by having sex, Doctor, never."

"*You* weren't hurt by it, perhaps. Not yet. The damage to Dexter still hasn't ended."

"Now, Doctor, what? Nothing has happened to him. He's . . . why, I understand that he's thriving."

"No he isn't. He's profoundly upset, his whole life has been turned upside down. Why, we were barely able to get his testimony. The boy. You should be glad you're not allowed to see him. It's a terrible thing."

It struck me in the gut, dropping the bottom out of all the conclusions I had made concerning him, my Dexter. How could he not be thriving? Certainly, I thought, his life must have continued, blossomed even, now without me. As difficult as that picture had been to conjure and accept, this new version, this suffering, his life turned upside down . . . it terrified me.

"What do you mean, Doctor? What's happened to him?"

"You still deny the tremendous vulnerability of the boy."

"But no, I don't, I've never. I always loved him precisely for it, his fragility."

"Yet you denied that your selfishness might damage someone so fragile."

"No, I would have known, he would have told me so."

"Well, it's all in the record now, in his testimony."

"His testimony, Doctor?"

"Against you, for the medical files."

"But, the trauma, if we'd not been torn apart."

"The damage would've simply been delayed, made worse in the end one must imagine."

"Delayed?"

"Until the point when he would manage to get away from you."

"But he didn't want to get away."

"Of course he didn't. This is one of your blind spots. So long as he was with you, he couldn't see how he was being hurt. Why, as is often the case, the boy even thought your molestations were a good, a desirable thing, so long as you were there in his life, blinding him, making him feel this sexual relationship was good for him."

"But I remember . . . he was so beautiful, so outspoken with me, telling me how he felt, good *and* bad. I never swayed him, no more than any lover sways the other . . . "

"The proof is in his anger now, just as I told you. Is it only coincidence that now, away from your influence, the boy is a wreck, devastated? This boy who you say was so capable and willing? Look at him now."

"I never forced . . . I was so frightened at first. I couldn't believe it when he kissed me, I even asked him to stop so I could think clearly. I, how could he be hurt so, or have wanted me? Doctor, where is he? I, can I help him?"

"No, you can't be allowed to see him. He's still terribly vulnerable, even more confused than before. Until he shows some sign of recognizing what you've done to him, some sign that he *can* protect himself, we won't let you see him. You've hurt this boy terribly. You'll just have to live with it."

I wanted only to find some way to make him better. Of course I thought of holding him, thinking of my sweet Dexter in pain, and of his hunger for love. I felt in my body the urge to soothe him, wrap him in my arms, caress and calm him. But my embrace was the weapon that had wounded him, my arms were black poison, selfish, blind serpents that wrecked the boy I had loved so deeply, the one whose fragility and courage had touched me at the bottom of my soul. I pulled them in tightly against myself, saving the world from their monstrous needs, and wept into my cotton bag. My Doctor-General sat in silent condemnation, letting me suffer my rain of tears.

Amid my snuffling and the rubbing of my cloth sack to dry my nose, he spoke up, offering guidance and counsel.

"You could take steps to save other boys from suffering the same fate, my friend. You could take real action against the weakness that has made you a danger."

"But, dear Doctor, I've tried, you know I've been sincere in my wish for our therapy to take hold. I fear I'm condemned to this, this deception where my soul cries love and I'm blind to the urge that's truly speaking."

"Organic steps. There are some things words can't cure."

"Drugs? I couldn't take drugs, not for the rest of my life."

"Surgery, my friend. Some operations are already viable."

"You could . . . cut it out?"

"I believe so. It would be a tremendous relief to you, I know it. I know in my heart you're sincerely remorseful. This simple option could take your hell away."

I listened as my Doctor-General rose from his chair and then sat beside me on the small couch. Silent and calm as Judas, he lifted the damp hem of my bag and kissed me, a gesture he'd begun on our very first day, but only now completed.

I nodded, slowly, and thought, yes, knowing now the cross I was to bear in this new life.

I'd never been so empty or helpless. My world was turned upside down, recast by the merciless truths of my Doctor-General. What I took to be love had been pain—blind pain which I'd poured down on my child, my lover. A kiss, an embrace, the working of his body to orgasm. I'd destroyed him utterly under the rain of my affections. What could ever come of deception except pain? What could any lie accomplish? Only to magnify the inevitable damage forced by the truth, by the day, somewhere coming, when the lie would turn over and reveal its underside, a dagger, an arrow, the sharp point calling my name.

My Doctor-General's confrontation might possibly have engendered hope if I'd come to any clear picture of the pattern and form of my self-deception. But I had none, not the slightest understanding of its modus operandi, its mysterious screens, gears turning silently inside me, dropping invisible scrims, casting the illusions so completely I still did not know the stage from reality. It was beyond me, the recognition of love, its separation from selfish desire. Could I ever trust the words of affection Hakan planted in my ear, wet, still, with his breath, his inquisitive tongue? What was I hearing? What was he saying, really? What would another man hear, free from the demonic misunderstandings that held reign in my head?

I felt as a shell, emptied of all but the stubborn afflictions that crawled and nested in the smallest hidden curl of my treacherous interior. My Doctor-General had turned me over and had shaken as hard as his unbridled words would allow, hoping to empty me, loosen these illusions from inside me until they dropped out dead, one by one, onto the floor. Yet he'd only succeeded in emptying my soul, leaving my barren spirit almost deserted, inhabited, now, only by deceptions, false faces, perilous masquerades.

I walked along the empty Avenue. The buntings had been mounted, the new banners hung. They beat against their stanchions, unseen in the black evening. The hills rose into the sky, standing silent above the city. Their lightless expanse stretched unbroken, crowding up against the factory gates. I traversed my beloved home, dwelling inside the contradictions of my life, the inheritance I'd come into, keen and eager child of the Ministry that now proposed to set me free. I hoped the knife might succeed in reshaping me, digging out that last bitter poison that words could not dislodge, making me fit, again, for the company of the children I loved with all my heart.

I opened the Salon door knowing I must be late. But I did not care, then, about the difficulties of my Prime Minister. A hole had been torn out inside me. The door of the Chamber was opened slightly. Its bright light poured into the hallway, casting grim shadows in the dust. He was sitting in the chair, his coat laid out beside him, inspecting his healthy face in the hand mirror. I knew I would grant him his new face now, if he would have it. I'd grown so weary of my labyrinthine deceptions. I had no will left to betray him.

"Mr. Sludge, I'm sorry you're late," he began, sounding a bit tender and embarrassed, like a caught child. "What seems to have delayed you?"

I could not comment, simply staring at him, my face reflecting the blankness of my heart. I sat in my stool, still dressed, maskless, with no tools or gown.

"I know who you are," I told him flatly. He was silent, unnerved, I guessed, more by my solemn affectless face than by my revelation. Perhaps he already knew. Surely he must have noticed, last time, my troubled recognition.

"Yes, well. Does it concern you at all?"

"A lot of people would like to find you."

He shifted in his chair, drawing his arms across his chest. The scraping of his soles across the linoleum betrayed his nervousness. "Yes, they would," he agreed. I stared without meaning to, without meaning anything. "I don't know that I would like to be found." He was an ice floe, an empty place in which a man had once dwelled. He seemed as insubstantial as air. He put his dry, thin hand to my shirt, undoing the buttons, and placed it on my heart.

"It's very strong, my friend." A warm shiver ran through me, beginning beneath his hand. My scalp tingled and my heart stirred, as though his weather were passing into me, lingering in his touch. I tried to speak, but my mouth and throat had gone dry.

"Yes, yes it is," I whispered.

"The skin is so soft." Now he whispered, the moment having taken his voice away. "I was young once," he breathed. His words were air. "My heart as strong as yours . . . a long time ago."

"Yes, yes you were." I had known it, sensing his youth, the long course of his life in the beating of his heart. I couldn't control my breathing, at once shallow and hard, as my leader's hand strayed, undoing the rest of my buttons.

"And powerful, whole armies, Mr. Sludge. Whole armies on their knees before me." The pageants, the photographs. His image swirled madly inside me, warmed by my sudden fever. His face, his proud strong breast, all puffed up and glorious, vivid in my memory. I closed my eyes, letting him drop his hands down into my lap. "Lay back, lay back beneath me," he commanded.

"Yes," I whispered, my trembling lips barely forming the simple sound. "Yes." The virgin skin of his face touched me, slipping down across my chest, the cheeks like velvet on my belly. My little friend rose to meet him, our leader, touching him upon the lips.

"Weeping, my friend. The sergeants wept upon my boots." He gasped and took me into his mouth, enclosing my tender sensitivity inside him, drawing me deep into his throat. I sang ecstatic within him . . . my leader, my Prime Minister. My lofty extension, inside his head, wiggling an inch further, impatient, pushing into him like a knife.

"Tears, tears ran across scuffed leather." He raised up for air and gasped his few words before taking me again. We beat as one, pulsing in each other's hearts, entangled upon the chair. The

Chamber and building, the streets and the cold night sky, the very city wrapped around us and framed my sacrifice. It is not enough to say I came; my spirit spilled out into his throat. That I emptied my sack into his gut is nothing beside the burden (and privilege) that was thus transferred to me. It would have been useless to refuse him.

He climbed off me, staggering a bit, and settled into the stool where I normally sat. Spent, I could not move from the chair. He stayed close by, leaning on the leather armrest, breathing unevenly. He seemed to wither where he sat, diminishing into himself as he rocked slightly back and forth. The night, behind a wall of stone, turned forward on its pivot. Our shallow breathing intermingled. What had passed, imprisoned in ourselves, between us?

"I can give you your face now, my Prime Minister," I finally whispered. "I'm sorry I delayed so long."

I reached above him to where the face lay, sheltered inside its wooden box. The latches had been disturbed, the velvet undone (certainly by him, in the few nervous moments before my coming in). I lifted the heavy lid, flipping it back on its hinges, and exposed the interior to his gaze. The face lay, silent among its braces, eyes turned away, its concavity opening toward us, hungry for the one to whom it would be wed.

He fidgeted where he sat. "You know I won't take it. Surely you've guessed that by now." The face lay before us like a curse, rebuilt and waiting. It needed only to be slipped on and fastened down.

"Like the last Prime Minister?" I asked, guessing at the origin of his long ordeal.

"Yes, I, I've been devoured by it. I have nothing left to give."

"Whose idea was it, then?" I imagined my leader acquiescent, granting his predecessor this gift, accepting the Byzantine plot, the balloon, the face, as he would the cross.

"His, the old man's. He couldn't go on. It would've been useless to refuse him."

"Your death was faked?"

"Yes, and the mask made mine. I didn't welcome it, not after what I'd seen it do to him."

I tried to imagine the genesis of the idea, the moment when our former leader saw in his young opponent the opportunity for escape. Wrung dry and empty, a tired old man (much like the man I now saw before me). The chance to pass his face on and flee must have been as a miracle, an intervention, a staying of his terrible sentence. "Where has he gone?" I asked.

"To Holland, he fled to Holland in disguise. I believe he's still there. You can't imagine the pain." His voice was tiny, almost imperceptible. It rattled like an infant wind deep in his occluded throat. "I'm a tired man, my friend. I don't think you can fully understand."

And what of the night that then engulfed him? What air filled its cold reaches, what weather crossed it? How endless was its extension, how awful the depth into which he then tumbled? Was it the same night as that within which his predecessor still wandered? Could children sleep in its embrace, or the moon crowd across its heavens? Could she be heard, her song drifting from the hills, or sung from the ship's bow; did it, oh heavenly sound, penetrate into those dark reaches? Everything came back wrong or impossible. The night into which he ran was deaf and blind, mute and lightless. He might have a life, again, elsewhere. But never again here, within the city.

I lay relaxed on the table, counting backward from one hundred as the man suggested. My body had been scrubbed all over and my gown loosened. I felt them lift it from me in the last moment before blackness descended and my life stopped, a blank

interlude of uncertain duration. It was unlike sleep or conscious-
ness of any kind that I have known. It began in that moment, the
surgical lights bright above me, and ended in a bed by a window,
the spring sun shining through the freshly washed panes, my
gown wrapped again around me, the room filled with fresh flowers.

I reached up to my head, hoping to feel somehow by its bandages, by the shape and shift of its surface, what magic had been
worked inside. Would there be scars? Inside as well as out?
Would anyone be able to tell, once my hair had grown back in?
Oddly, I felt no different. No beatific haze had descended, no
empty apathy, as I'd secretly feared. My head was bare, the stub-
ble still short and bristly, no bandages fastened there. I wondered
what miraculous technique my Doctor-General had devised,
allowing him entry into that most interior place without violation of my skull. Perhaps it was one of Dr. Freeman's innovations,
one of those thin, sort of ice picks the doctor merely jams in over
the eye. I patted around, feeling for sore spots or bruises, but
found none.

It was a comfort. The mess and violence of my Doctor-General's experimentations had almost been enough to put me off
the cure. As late as the hour before my surgery I'd thought I
might call it off, fleeing from the unknown, seeking sanctuary in
the more familiar hell in which I'd dwelled all my life. But I swallowed my fears, remembering with bitter clarity the depth of my
sadness over Dexter.

A nurse came in, bearing sponges and antiseptic on a little
chrome tray. She was surprised to find me awake.

"And how are we today?" this little angel cooed, obviously well
practiced in her bedside manner. "Feeling any pain, are we?"

"No, no I'm not, thank you, nurse." I patted about my head
blindly. "Not even able to find the scar, for that matter." She gig-

gled at my demonstrations, dousing the sponge with a splash of antiseptic.

"Oh, now, now. You needn't be coy with me. I'm a trained nurse, you know, used to far more delicate matters than this." She lifted my gown. "We'll just be washing it up. Can't be too careful." She dabbed the heavy sponge against my shaven testicles. I looked on, stunned. My bare body was splotched with blushing patches where they'd shaved me. A small, almost invisible scar ran across the loose folds of my scrotum. She lifted and touched it, cleaning each crevice thoroughly, but I felt nothing, no pain or excitement. Nothing.

The ship left the harbor in the dusk of one evening, Lucrezia standing amidships. The glory of her wardrobe flew in the wind, fastened to the ship's upper rigging. She sang, I'm told, a last time as the ship went to sea with her, destined for Dutch soil and her life in exile. Hakan explained it to me, teary-eyed and uncomprehending the first time I saw him after my absence (the purpose of which I had left unexplained).

"They've gone," he repeated. "They've left us just before the Festival, our triumph. They've taken it." I comforted him, cuddling him close to my body, clumsy and apologetic about my lack of enthusiasm, blaming it on the sadness of his tale.

"I should've known," I told him. "She couldn't simply go on performing in that zoo the rest of her life."

"But she would have been triumphant," he blubbered. "The opera house, it could've been hers." Perhaps so, I thought, depending on what that madman, our former leader, had planned. Perhaps he'd returned from Holland simply to smuggle her away? Obviously he had no other grand designs (or had decided against them after arriving). My head was over full with resolutions, final good-byes. I held Hakan with nostalgia in my arms, not passion.

Something strange and subtle had been cut out of me. It hadn't removed my love, nor my desire, really, for his affections. It simply robbed me of the means by which to act on it. Desire burned in me still, a troubling, inextinguishable flame. But its connection to the outer shell of my body had been severed, mangled and numbed, so that the actions I expected, the loving expression of that interior fire, never materialized.

"The opposition leader made it to shore," I told him. "I've seen him at the Salon. Disguised, just as you predicted."

Hakan looked at me, unwilling to believe, to rethink the future of his world in light of so drastic a turn. "You, why haven't you told anyone?"

"That's why I went away. I followed him, I found him. He's willing. And the Prime Minister has agreed."

"The Prime Minister will step down? You've kept him from his face?" Hakan's eyes moved rapidly back and forth, sweeping across me as if searching for a lie, a flaw, any hidden trap that might upset the tremendous enthusiasms he was now rebuilding.

"The Prime Minister was eager. He wanted only to get out. I've arranged for you to meet the new Prime Minister, your man." I held my tears back, realizing the depth of his affection for this enigmatic, elusive figure. "You must help him, he'll be expecting you." I couldn't enjoy the terrible embraces my blessed boyfriend now gave me. They were abstracted thoughts, neutral gestures occurring around me.

I embraced him once more, through the prison wall that had descended inside me, trapping my mind in its paradoxical interior. "I'll be leaving," I told him. "I can't stay."

I'll spare you the words and kisses he troubled me with, using terms like love and need as though he had any comprehension of them. I'll spare you the deceptive entreaties he made, protestations, echoing Dexter in the confusion of his moment, laying traps into which, only days ago, I might have fallen. I'll spare you the pain that racked my heart with every word he said, every moment he held me, and the tears he cried. Treacherous lies that had damned me once before. I could only walk away from them.

I opened the Chamber door and took the box down from its place. The latches were still undone, the top slightly shifted off its base. I opened it. The face lay upside down, its emptiness pointed toward me. I slipped it on, pressing its supple edges down where they would mesh, soon, with my own skin, working the interior around so that it fit snugly against me. It felt like water, or air, suffering against my face. I'd grow used to it soon enough. It might even be good for me. I'd seen what beautiful skin it had given to the last man who wore it.

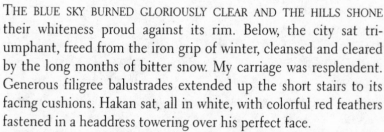

THE BLUE SKY BURNED GLORIOUSLY CLEAR AND THE HILLS SHONE their whiteness proud against its rim. Below, the city sat triumphant, freed from the iron grip of winter, cleansed and cleared by the long months of bitter snow. My carriage was resplendent. Generous filigree balustrades extended up the short stairs to its facing cushions. Hakan sat, all in white, with colorful red feathers fastened in a headdress towering over his perfect face.

He faced back, and I climbed aboard opposite him. Oh, how he loved his leader, the image of his leader (though he would never know it was I, locked within). His love was distant and supplicating, the sort of worship befitting a eunuch.

We rode through the crowded streets. Bells rang from every tower, filling the sweet spring air, echoing and calling across the length of our city. I was attended by advisors, a retinue about which I'd known nothing, busy men with clipboards and lenses, light meters hung round their necks like rosaries. They'd been my constant companions since the very first, when I'd arrived by taxi at the Prime Ministerial palace.

"At last," the balding chief advisor had barked, greeting me in the Great Hall. Would he detect my masquerade? I kept my posture, drawing myself out, allowing not even a thought to expose itself through the mask. Did the Prime Minister speak much? No, I thought not. Terse, gruff greetings. An air of power, resolve. Take charge, orchestration through invisible signals. I exposed my boot, taking a deep breath, and extended it toward him, ready to receive his kiss.

"Look, whoever you are," he said, grasping my shoulder with a chummy hand, "we've only got a few hours. I need you dressed and ready by five, and your blocking memorized. Don't fuck up on me now, you understand? Toby!" he called out, gesturing to a fat man hovering near the ballroom door. "Toby, get her out of these rags and into the red number. Check with me when you're ready, got it?"

"Toby" scurried off, bowing and scraping, and I was ushered into a small bedroom where I sat alone. A plate of chocolates had been left, and an ice bucket. I pulled a frosty decanter of pear juice from it and sipped. My impotence was something of a relief. I had no idea what I'd have done had the Palace received me in chaos, frenzied ministers begging me for advice and directions. What would I have said? My dressers arrived, tugging my civilian garments off me and stuffing me into "the red number." It was fabulous, easily the equal of anything I'd seen before at the pageants (*or* at the Burlesque). They didn't speak, manipulating me by firm pushes and pulls, much like the barber or dentist does, indicating the particular tilt of the head with silent hands. The Chief Advisor reappeared.

"So, doll, speak to me," he bade, addressing, I believe, me. "Tell me what you think."

"About the dress?"

"Of course about the dress. What else?" He pressed his light meter close to my skin.

"It's very nice, Mr., uh."

"Mel, honey, just Mel. Toby," he barked again. Evidently the rooms were wired for sound, like the laboratory of Flessinger and Ponz. "Toby, get me some powder, will you? She's too shiny." He turned back toward me and smiled. "Speak to me, baby. What do you need?"

"Well, I wonder about my speech. Shouldn't I have some paper, to jot a few notes?"

"Nervous, doll? Don't be, leave it to me, will you." He primped my gown, puffing the sleeves out, and sprayed them with some sort of aerosol fixer. "Hold it, now, don't breathe," he cautioned. "Nasty stuff." The sticky mist settled, invisibly fixing the fabric in a thin shellac. "Don't move those arms now, doll, you'll crack."

"But, uh, Mel, what about the speech?" I felt faint and dizzy from the fumes. "May I sit?"

"Hold it. Grip!" he shouted. "Two, please, pronto." Two beefy young men burst through the door, breathless and dim-witted. "Prop her up, will ya, she needs a rest." My attendants wedged themselves in behind me, lifting me comfortably aloft in my recline, straight and still so my dress wouldn't crack. "Better?" Mel asked brightly.

It was better. Alas, I felt myself disappearing, and worried that I might never wear my own clothes again. It took my breath away. Where was I?

"The speech, baby," Mel's distant voice intoned. "Don't worry about the speech. We'll have it piped in." I listened dumbly, supine upon my human bier, and sweated into my gown. It would be better once we got outside, the carriage, the bracing breeze upon the dais.

"Piped in, Mel?" I wheezed, feverish.

"Oh yeah, doll, the best. We use it every year. Toby!" Mel banged his fist against his ear, evidently correcting some malfunction in the mechanism. "Toby, wire up the tapes. What's that? Flowers, my man, some sort of bouquet to block her mouth. No, Toby, no she can't just move her lips."

He drifted away, or I did, lost among the mountains to the east, mixing with the smoke of the rebel fires, the factory ash, the great exhalations of the city.

I sparkled upon the dais, awash in bright sunlight and the adoration of my people. Festive bunting framed me, my heavy dress and the weight of my miter. Invisible props kept me standing, aloft and triumphant. Around my feet tunicked children knelt, while beside me my favorite, Hakan, stood proud and clean, shining like a brightly washed bauble. His fine dark hair, released from its ceremonial decoration, feathered in the brisk wind. He gazed in adoration at my mask and could not, would not, see through it. He had never loved me more.

The Prime Minister's voice surrounded us, ringing off the ancient walls of our city, blessing us all inside by its benediction. It echoed from the citadel, sounding in the empty university halls. It announced itself, touching the church towers, reflected from the opera's golden dome. It was the clouds and wind, the freshness of our new spring. I turned my face to the exalted skies and gestured mutely, marking the meter of his words.